Paradox Unbound

D1523151

Grant Cain

Contents

CHAPTER 1

The Side Project

"What are you working on?" Evan asked, plopping his backpack on the worn, light blue couch. "And why are you using my tools again?"

"Side project," Benny answered, raising his head slightly to acknowledge Evan's existence. "And it's not like you use them anymore." Evan knew exactly what Benny meant when he said "Side project"; he was tampering with something he shouldn't be.

"Doesn't mean you can just use them. You are replacing anything that gets broken you know."

"With what money?" Benny had to laugh at himself.

Evan chuckled a bit too, although he hated himself for it just a bit. Ever since they were roommates at the start of college, Benny had always taken advantage of the "benefits of friendship" as he called it. Now that they were juniors and had lived together for three years, the benefits seemed to be used much more than they used to be.

"Okay, what are you trying to blow up this time?" Evan inquired.

"Let me see your MEBA."

"Heck no!"

"And why not?"

"How many MEBAs have you had to buy new parts for?"

Benny was quiet, turning back to his workbench and started fiddling again.

[Mechanical Entry of Biological Adjustments (or MEBAs for short) had changed the way everyone lived ever since they were invented fifteen years ago. Neuro-Psychologist Dr. Wilfred Raffe had found that the physiological response of the human body could be tracked to capture data isolating the feelings of guilt. In working with the government around the world, he had developed devices small enough to be inserted into every person at the base of the heart, where it received signals from the amygdala to pump blood faster. Suddenly, the government had a surefire way to determine guilt. They quickly put the MEBA system into place. MEBAs were small, fist-sized displays issued to people when they are born. The MEBA lights would shine either red or blue and would adjust to the successes/mistakes people made. Each minute, it reported the firing of specific chemicals and electric pulses in the brain to a worldwide network, giving a score out of 100 to inform the person where they stood in their "moral code". The more red lights, the more mistakes someone had made based on their levels of guilt. The more blue lights, the more honorable the deeds someone had done. Many big businesses and corporations backed the idea immediately, as it allowed them insight into the right person to hire as well as identifying internal corporate crimes. There was initial upheaval in many areas of government, religion, business, and education, but after a couple of years, the previously shocking stories stopped being so shocking. Dr. Raffe was given the Nobel Peace Prize for his invention and more money than he knew what to do with.

Economies began to boom under the government's more watchful eye and regulations. Since many countries quickly adopted the technology, the United Nations began collaborating on more diverse and worldwide topics. But those were the stories of fifteen years ago. By now, it had become commonplace. Frantic workers, teenagers, and spouses checked their MEBAs every few hours or so just to make sure scores hadn't changed.]

Evan grabbed a box of cheese snacks and a spot on the couch next to his backpack. Reaching for the remote, he turned on the tv and switched the channel from whatever violent cartoons Benny had on from that morning to the news, which, as usual, was discussing lowered crime rates and new technology.

"Please watch anything but the news," Benny pleaded with his friend.

"Why do you hate the news so much?"

"I don't hate it. It's just boring"

"Everything is boring to you."

"You make it sound like it's my fault for being a genius," Benny smirked as a couple of sparks jumped from his MEBA in front of him.

Evan just ignored him, as good friends tend to do after coming to a point in the conversation where both sides know what the other is going to say. The news team smiled happily as they reported on the feel-good story of the day: a man had made a citizen's arrest of someone who was trying to hack into the government database and change his MEBA results.

"Jack Charles, the citizen that made the arrest, now sports a wonderful MEBA of 96 thanks to his heroic deeds," the television chirped happily.

"96!" Evan spat, freeing a few of the crumbs that had gathered on his lower lip.

"Big deal," Benny had to have the last word between the two.

"It is a big deal. The guy could probably walk into any company he wants and get an upper level management job with that kind of score. Highest I've ever gotten mine is freakin' 68. I'm pissed. Never gonna be able to get that high in time for graduation. Heck, 70 is barely enough these days to get a decent paying job."

"Especially if you keep changing your major and never graduate college," another smirk. "What are you studying THIS week?"

"Microbiology." By this he meant Microbiology and Tech, but no one ever said "and tech" anymore. Everyone majored in technology because it was frowned upon to not have a technology degree.

"Oh puh-leese. What are you going to do with a major like that?"

A pause lingered as Evan tried to think of something. "Not sure yet."

Evan's MEBA, always clipped to his side, flashed something he knew wasn't normal. Glancing at it, it's glowing lights spelled out "hi". He whipped his head toward Benny, sporting a scowl. "This better not be you."

"Well hello to you too!" He grinned through his chapped lips. Holding up his MEBA, which also said "hi."

4

"Why do I even bother?" Evan asked the room, because he knew the answer Benny was going to give.

"Because you love me." They said together, Evan rolling his eyes in the process. He then continued, "have you at least studied for the Bio-Mechanical test yet?"

"Who would dare give us a test right before Thanksgiving?"

"Professor Tile."

"How dare she!" the sarcasm dripped from Benny's mouth. "Doesn't she know who I am!?"

"Everyone in class knows who you are loudmouth." Evan sighed. Every day was the same witty banter, but there was comfort in it. He honestly wouldn't know what to do if he and Benny didn't live together; ever since they met in school and argued over which girl they thought was prettier (Benny somehow won that argument too), the two haven't been apart more than a few days. People would comment behind their backs about how weird it was that they were always hanging out, but they were both mature enough not to care. Benny appreciated that about Evan, but it was always an unspoken appreciation.

After a yawn, Benny got up from his workbench. "Well, I'm going to bed."

"It's 3:30," Even stated, then emphasized, "PM."

"Didn't sleep last night. Too busy working on the MEBA."

"You spent all night working just so you could send me a 2 letter word on my MEBA?!"

"No," Benny chuckled. "That only took me about 5 minutes to figure out."

"What was the other," Evan took a second to calculate, "seven hours spent on?"

"Side project," the door closed behind him and Evan heard the soft thump of a body hitting a bed a few seconds later.

"Benny! Tampering with your MEBA is illegal!" Evan made sure his roommate could hear him over the fake snoring he was giving off. "You know how much trouble you can get in for tampering with your MEBA!" He looked down for a second, his MEBA flashing a winking face back at him. "AND MINE!"

* * *

"You're gonna be late," Evan shouted to Benny.

"Fine with me," Benny said, giving away that he was awake. "Tile's tests aren't too bad."

Evan gave a sigh. He had begun struggling recently with Tile's class. Through high school, he was an A-student who always got the subject material the first try. He knew he was smart and it frustrated him all the more to find that such a seemingly simple class turned sour as his grades did. Asking for help was even worse. A couple of weeks ago, he slipped into Professor Tile's office in hopes of figuring out what it was that was stumping him.

"Good morning Mr. Roman," her British accent rounded off some of the words. She smiled a big, seemingly genuine smile. Tile was a visiting professor last year, but stayed on full time when a position opened up. Delvedale Technical School had always been a smaller school with smaller classes in a small Georgia town. It made for classes with no more than forty people, allowing the teachers and students to at least be familiar with each other. Tile had stayed because she appreciated the less busy environment. In addition, Delvedale had become an important name recently as two of their former professors had some incredible breakthroughs in their fields and became world famous for supporting and helping the MEBA project. It was their positions that Tile had come in to fill at the last minute. "How are you today?"

"I don't know," Evan said sheepishly. "How does tutoring usually work?"

"Well, usually the student warns me ahead of time, or at least comes during my office hours. It is eight in the morning you know."

"Sorry, I'll come back later."

"No, it's fine," Tile invited him in. "What part of the coursework are you struggling with?" Evan told her and they spent the next hour or so starting from the beginning of the section. Only near the end of the hour did Evan realize that Tile was much more friendly in person than in front of a class. She made him a cup of tea, which he liked very much, and patiently walked him through the process of breaking down the difficult topic of bio-nanobots. "I think you've just about got it," she said as they finished up. "Let me know if you need any more help. You are a smart kid, Mr. Roman. I think you can do great things in this field. Just remember that the origin of the technology always sets the stage for the constants used in the classroom."

"Thank you, Professor Tile," he started getting up. "I'll come in if I need any more help going forward." And he did. Tile quickly became his favorite professor. Even after he understood the material, he would stroll into her office again and again just to ask additional questions or get a cup of tea. She never turned him away. It made Evan more and more excited to go to her class. It even started to get on his nerves that Benny had so little interest in what he considered a fascinating course.

The test wasn't particularly hard for Evan and he was excited to brag to Benny on the way back. Benny smirked as Evan recounted the two questions he wasn't really sure about.

"I made a 100." Benny said nonchalantly.

"How do you know?" Evan immediately argued.

"Other than the fact that the material was easy? Well in case you haven't noticed, Tile always does her answers in a pattern."

"She does?"

"Yep," Benny grinned. "It's always a different pattern for each test, but once you figure it out, it's simple to go back and check your answers to the pattern. This one was CDCBAD." Evan thought for a bit at this information. He wouldn't use it to do better, but it was interesting. He then realized he may have gotten the last problem wrong.

"Wait, isn't the last question A?" Evan asked. "That would fall out of the pattern!"

"Oh yeah, her last answer is always 37. Haven't you noticed? Not sure why, but I think it's to catch people who figure out the pattern to see if they are really paying attention. It was a dead giveaway on this test too. You could tell she phrased the question to make the answer 37. Why else would she say 'how many thousands of nanobots are released?' instead of just saying 'how many nanobots are released?' and making the answer 37,000? She's an odd one for sure." Benny laughed to himself.

"She is not odd," Evan defended his favorite teacher. "She just does things a little differently."

"Uh huh," Benny was clearly tired from having to wake up in the middle of his sleeping time "just to take a test".

When the boys made it back to their dorm room, Evan grabbed the remote, snatched the remaining cheese snacks, and flipped on the news; Benny complained about the tv on his way to his workbench.

Sitting back on his couch and wishing he had a cup of tea, Evan took a look at his MEBA, which read 61. He hadn't looked at it for a couple of days, but he was surprised to see it fall a few spots. Had he done something wrong? Was finding out the information about the pattern a bad thing even if he wasn't going to act on it? How was he supposed to correct it? He wasn't sure; all he knew was that he didn't want to take a hit in his MEBA rating because of something he didn't know was wrong. He hadn't even felt guilty about anything.

"Hey Benny," Evan called out. "Has your MEBA score changed recently?

"Nope, why?"

"Mine when down a little bit, but I don't know why. When you messed with my MEBA the other day, do you think that would have changed anything?"

"Dunno," Benny didn't care to solve this mystery, keeping his eyes on his tinkering.

"My parents aren't gonna like this. Dad always tells me that this is the time I should be doing more charity work or something else that usually increases scores. I never feel like I have time though."

"You'd have more time if you watched less news," Benny grinned wide, knowing that he "got" his roommate. Ever since they started being roommates, Benny had always gotten the best of Evan. Evan always seemed to have great ideas, but they always got shot down or dismissed as something that would never work. At first, Evan hated it and nearly asked for a roommate change because he was frustrated by how often it happened. However, the more Evan got to know Benny, the more he realized that the comments he made weren't made to make him feel bad, but rather to support him. He recognized that if he took Benny's advice, he tended to have better days and understood both his school and his family better. He had come to respect all of the comments, even if they were made as a joke.

Benny, however, had liked Evan from the beginning. He immediately recognized that Evan was a "good kid" from a "good family" that always worked hard. He appreciated that and made sure to mention when Evan did something really well. Benny liked that he and his roommate would stay up late at night and talk for hours about anything and everything. Evan's questions were always welcomed in the conversations, despite Benny always seeming to have the right answer or at least one that made him feel right to Evan. Occasionally, Evan would stick to whatever opinion he had in their conversations, even if Benny tried to correct him. Those interactions always led to quieter nights or fewer conversations later on, at least until Evan found out that Benny was right, the latter never purposefully rubbing it in Evan's face.

Evan turned the volume on the TV up some more so he could hear better, the caption at the bottom of the screen catching his eye.

"Can you turn that down? I'm trying to focus." Benny snapped at his roommate.

"Have you seen this yet?" Evan redirected Benny's short attention span.

On the news there was an story that had broken that morning. The newscaster gave a stern stare as he reported:

"In international news. A girl from Cambridge passed away this morning. After her death, investigators found that she had been connected to an underground anti-government group known as the Exodus. Detective Robert Barnes, an expert in psychology and networking of anti-government movements, stated that there was no hard evidence that enabled them to discover any locations where the group had met or where they might meet next. The team of investigators believes that the deceased, one Amelia Rose, had recently joined the group. When her guilt caused her MEBA score to drop rapidly, she overdosed on her mother's medication and her heart stopped. Detective Barnes is tightening his focus on the Cambridge campus, where he believes many of her fellow Exodus members may reside. Many are calling this unfortunate loss a success for recent MEBA studies and their ability to help regulate gang-related affairs."

The news story had made Evan feel even more concerned for himself and how he had lost a few dots on his own MEBA.

"Sounds bogus," Benny scoffed.

"What do you mean?" Evan replied.

"Of all the things happening in the world, why make a news story out of that? Why not talk about war or how the protests against new data research are keeping scientists in their homes? Focusing on one girl who may or may not be connected to one of the probably hundreds of anti-government factions just doesn't make any sense."

"Oh," Evan hadn't really thought about it. "Yeah, I guess."

Benny just laughed and turned back to his work. A few moments later, the lights overhead flickered. "Eureka!" He shouted.

"Should I ask?"

"Of course you should. You are among the great men of our generation." His cocky voice had come back on. "Take a look."

Evan did so. But when he held Benny's MEBA up, there was nothing on it.

"Where are the dots?" He asked. "How can you tell your score?"

"Exactly," Benny beamed.

CHAPTER 2

Family and Secrets

Thanksgiving at the Roman household was fairly typical. The food was fatty and delightful, the conversations were always a little awkward, but loving and pleasant. Evan had a large family, six in total. Jillian, being the eldest by four years, had already graduated college and was working at the local animal shelter in hopes of starting her own someday. After Jillian and Evan was Roxanne (she went by Roxie most of the time), who was born two years after Evan and had started college this year.

Their parents had made quite a bit of money as stock brokers and it had made life easy for them as the years went on. By the time Jillian had gotten to college, the large, old house they had lived in for over a decade had begun to feel empty; they adjusted this by adopting the 9-year old boy of a family they had known and grown close to through their church. The parents had suffered a fatal boating accident, leaving the 9-year old with only his elderly grandmother to take care of him, a task she was not physically able to do. The Romans had known the Michaels for a long time and had practically helped them raise their son Jeremy; it was normal for them to give the Michaels parenting advice, old parenting books, and have their kids babysit whenever the Michaels needed a night off. Jeremy was a tough kid to take care of though, having many problems at birth and being sickly until he turned four. This just made the Romans all the more passionate about taking care of him after the tragedy.

It was a tough transition for Jeremy to move in with them; it happened right as Evan was entering high school. As soon as Evan learned to drive at fourteen, he would take Jeremy out to get ice cream once a week (paid for by mom and dad usually). When they were younger, this was often a time where Evan would get to sit and listen to whatever his new brother wanted to say. Jeremy never really opened up about his parents very well, but he never minded talking either. Mostly the conversation was about school, or toys, or kids he didn't like. Evan would get a few words in when Jeremy was licking his banana cream cone, but the talking tended to be one-sided. He liked it that way. He learned so much about Jeremy that he began to feel like a third parent to him.

When Evan left for college, he gave Jeremy his access key to his personal high school database and a thumbprint to unlock it. When Jeremy made it to high school at 13, he would be able to see all of the work his older brother had done. This Thanksgiving was the first time they had seen each other since he had opened his brother's database and all Jeremy wanted to talk about was what he had found there. During the big feast, Evan could tell Jeremy was excited, so he asked if he wanted to go for a walk after they ate. Jeremy beat him out the door.

"So how is Corville High?" Evan asked as they turned down the driveway.

"It's fine I guess," Jeremy's voice had changed quite a bit in the last couple of years. "I have your old math teacher."

"Finnegan?"

"Yeah, he's hilarious."

"Has he done the ventriloquist act yet?"

"The talent show is next week. I'm gonna be in it."

"Really?" Evan was actually surprised. "What are you doing?"

"The choir teacher put a group of us together to sing a couple songs. There are only six of us so I guess that means I'm pretty good." He gave a proud little grin.

"Better not let your voice squeak during the talent show."

"I'll do my best," Jeremy spoke in a very low tone as a joke. Evan gave him a courtesy laugh.

"You'll do fine."

"So, I looked into your database."

"Yeah? Did you like it?"

"It's amazing!"

Evan blushed a little. "Which part is your favorite?"

"I really like the 3D art project you made.

"Oh yeah, I for…."

"And the vocal command robot you programmed," Jeremy interrupted. "And the auto-tuned theater production. What class was that for? It wasn't under a specific teacher."

Evan chuckled. "It wasn't for a class. I actually just did it in my spare time when I was bored. Thought it would be funny. I leaked it to the main server at school so that anyone could access it. It was almost a prank, but not mean enough I suppose." Jeremy laughed, and Evan was glad to see that high school had not been too rough in his absence. Jeremy still had that youthful innocence about him and his curiosity seemed to make him a great student.

"Hey, what was up the with the corrupted file?"

"What corrupted file?"

"There is a file that I can't get into. Says it was corrupted or something."

"Don't remember anything like that. I'll take a look when we get home."

They took another lap around the neighborhood and cut through the nearby soccer field when the wind started picking up. It looked as though it was bringing storm clouds with it. When the boys got home, there was peach pie coming out of the oven, filling the air with a delightful scent of cinnamon and fresh baked butter-crust. When they had shoved the warm slices into their mouths, the family went to watch a movie together in the living room. The boys knew that they couldn't get out of it; tradition is tradition. The entire time the movie was on, Evan kept thinking about the corrupted file and trying to figure out what Jeremy was talking about. He checked his MEBA during the movie, holding it in such a way that only he could see it. 54. It was plummeting and he didn't know why.

As soon as the movie was over, he and Jeremy went up to Jeremy's room (it was Evan's old room) to check out the database. Accessing the files from high school was so strange for Evan. After seeing the direction that technology was headed, the methods and tools used in high school seemed so old-fashioned. Bringing up the list of classes and teachers under his personal profile brought back many happy memories, and a few tough ones. He made it to the files for class projects and started scrolling through them. Sure enough, near the bottom, there was a file that had been corrupted. Had he been hacked? Was this related to his MEBA score? Should he tell the Tech Bureaux so they could look into the problem?

"See?" Jeremy was looking over his brother's shoulder.

"Yeah, that's weird alright," Evan replied.

"What class would that have been?"

Evan started looking through the coding for the file itself. It was fairly easy to crack and he even used some of the things he had recently learned in his tech security class to pass over the locks in the way. For the first time, he had felt like an actual hacker; it felt good to put some of his learning to use, even if it was for something that typically frowned upon. He knew how dangerous hacking could be as a profession and that many of them end up with low MEBA scores and can't find other work, but he threw logic out the window in this moment to satisfy his curious nature. It felt like driving down the highway for the first time; his blood pumped faster as he drew close to figuring out exactly what was happening. He didn't believe in conspiracies, but was feeling like the world was working against him. Three more firewalls. Jeremy leaned in closer. Two more. A quick panic darted through his head telling him to stop, but he was too close. One more. The last security measure on the file was a passcode. Evan tried his old high school password. It didn't work. Maybe the one he used from college? Nope. He wished he had a de-scrambling device to figure the password out for him.

"Sorry bud," Evan finally gave up. "I can't get into it tonight. Too many guesses could flag the system and make this problem much worse."

"What problem?" Jeremy had not been inside Evan's head the past few minutes.

"It's nothing." Evan avoided eye contact, feeling a little bit weird how much he enjoyed trying to hack into the corrupted file. Hopefully, he thought to himself, it didn't lower his MEBA score any more.

The rest of the Thanksgiving Break went quickly. Evan's parents announced to the family that they were planning on opening up an orphanage in South America and that, even though it would take a while, they were really excited about it. They were going to make some trips this year and take Jeremy with them to scout out a few areas and get a better feel for where they wanted to open the orphanage. Jillian offered to help when her work allowed, and Roxie slyly mentioned that her new boyfriend loves to travel. She was brutally questioned about this boyfriend in a way that only family can.

* * *

The radio in Evan's car was busted a year ago when Benny got upset about an interview they were listening to and "accidentally" hit it with a hammer. Despite this, time with his family had always lifted Evan's spirits, even to the point where a two hour drive back to campus seemed like a two minute drive down the street. As he parked, he noticed a bright blue convertible in Benny's spot. The top covered the light tan leather from the harsh wind that was blowing that morning. At first glance, Evan thought Benny had made some shady exchange over the break; he then noticed that the license plate was from Florida. He figured it must just be someone visiting with a friend who didn't know that Benny had a short fuse about keeping his parking spot open when he wasn't there. As he headed to the stairs that led to their room, empty box after empty box greeted him, waving their cardboard flaps in the breeze. As he came to the door, he almost ran into a guy carrying yet another box.

"Sorry about that," he said in a voice that despite Evan's good spirits somehow made him suddenly feel sour. Evan couldn't help but twinge at how raspy it was. His cheery thanksgiving mood had been broken quickly.

"No problem," Evan gritted his teeth. "Who are you?" He couldn't think of a nice way of telling this intruder to leave.

"I'm your new roommate. The name is Hank, but my friends call me Cream."

Evan started staring at the guy's bright white hair and the blonde roots, evidence of dyeing it a few weeks ago. It hung down to his neck in a way that Evan assumed was because he was a surfer or at least wanted to look like one. Even though he had nothing against that lifestyle, Evan immediately took to disliking the stranger.

"What do you mean new roommate?" He asked with anger spilling out from his tongue. "Where is Benny?"

"I'm guessing he was the guy that left?" Cream asked back. "No idea. I've been on a waiting list for this school for a while now, and they just called to let me know there was an open spot, so I came."

Something didn't sit right in Evan's head. Benny didn't call, or text, or leave a weird cryptic note for him to decipher. He was usually a bit unpredictable, but this would be a new level for him. He immediately tried to text him, but received an error message from the phone company, saying that the number did not exist. When he went into the living room to drop off the clothes he had worn while he was home, he noticed that the work bench Benny spent so much time at was suspiciously clean. Evan started poking around like a detective in his own home, looking for something to tip him off to what had happened. Unable to find anything important, he went out to clear his head. At this point, Evan figured he wouldn't be able to do anything about Cream anyway, so talking to him while he unpacked his convertible felt unproductive. He started walking the empty sidewalks that traversed campus, hoping to make some sense of his friend's sudden absence. He took out his MEBA; 42. He shuddered. What he didn't realize was that he naturally started walking towards Professor Tile's office without noticing. When he reached her building, he poked his head in to see if she was even back from her break yet.

"Well good morning Mr. Roman," her accent brought a little bit of comfort to Evan's wandering mind. "How was your Thanksgiving?"

"Can I bother you?" he asked sheepishly.

"Of course you can."

"Do you know what happened with Benny?"

"What do you mean?"

"Apparently, he is no longer going here."

"That doesn't seem right. Did he say anything about leaving?"

"Not a thing." Both of them thought about this for a second.

Tile unlocked her lowest desk drawer and pulled a small device from it. The device was black with five slightly glowing buttons. She tapped on a few of them, turned back to Evan, and continued inquiring. "Did he do anything that may have been dangerous to himself or to others?"

"What's that thing for?"

"Nothing for now."

Evan sat and thought. He can't just tell her that Benny would fiddle illegally with his MEBA, trying new programs and possibly erasing his MEBA score. She would be forced to take the information to the authorities, which could already be worse than whatever pickle he found himself in this time. Dr. Tile picked up on Evan's worried face. Getting very serious all of the sudden, she repeated herself.

"Evan, did Benny do something dangerous or illegal?"

"I think so," the words dribbled out of Evan's mouth, hitting the floor with a thud. He felt relieved for some reason, not realizing how much of a toll it had taken to keep his old roommate's messy lifestyle a secret.

"Tell me about it."

Evan did, and felt comfortable doing so. He didn't think that he was ratting out his friend and could only hope that Tile would understand his confusion.

"How long has he been tinkering illegally for?"

"Ever since I've known him."

"What was the last thing he was working on?"

21

"I think he was trying to erase his MEBA score without an alert on the system, like an EMP device or something."

Tile leaned forward, suddenly much more interested. "Did he succeed?"

"Yeah, I think so, just before the break. He was really excited." The moment seemed to drag on as Tile began processing and thinking about what she should do or say. Evan eventually broke the silence. "What should we do?"

The teacher looked her student straight in the eye, her countenance had become even more serious and sort of dark, as though a cloud had come into the room to dim everything. She whispered quietly to Evan. "Benny is a brilliant kid. If he really did find a way to send a signal from his MEBA that would alter its feedback to fit his own desires, it would be the first backdoor into that system since it was created. What he created is incredibly powerful and you can bet that incredibly powerful people have been more than keeping an eye on him."

Evan stared blankly, not fully understanding the weight of the situation. "So why make him disappear?" He asked, lowering his voice as well.

"The system in place is one of control, one that gives appropriate consequences for positive and negative actions. Benny has learned how to override the control they have with the flip of a switch. He has made himself the thing that the system most fears."

"A rogue? Some type of renegade?"

"A free man. Someone unable to be seen or understood by the system of right and wrong they have established. He has made himself unpunishable for his actions."

"If that got out, there would be no way to tell right from wrong."

"At least according to the MEBA system and the AMA." Professor Tile was of course referring to the Agency of MEBA Affairs, the business group that monitored and regulated the MEBA system.

"Ok, so what can we do?"

"Nothing. If they found out what Benny did and brought him in for questioning, there is no telling where he is now. He could already have been locked up, forced to give them his information, or worse."

"Well I doubt he would tell them anything."

"Then most likely they are going to try to reverse engineer the coding and technology he made."

"How long do you think it could take?"

"Knowing Benny, it could be weeks, even months."

"Do you think we could find him?"

"Not without a clue as to where he is."

"So what are we supposed to do?" Evan was upset and his voice picked up. "Just let them do whatever they want and go about our business?"

"Keep a low profile for now. If they were keeping tabs on Benny, they may have been keeping tabs on you. If I'm ever not at class, you may as well suspect that they have taken me in for questioning.

Benny was my student after all. Don't do or say anything that you think may put you under suspicion. We just have to hope that he is okay. Remember, if he is the only one to make a backdoor to the MEBA statistics, they need him until they get what they want."

Evan agreed. This was definitely the biggest mess Benny had gotten him in. He turned to walk out the door, only to remember about his personal MEBA score. "Hey Professor Tile?"

"Yes?"

He suddenly realized that he wasn't even sure if he could trust her. What if the only reason they found Benny was because of him? Was it his fault for talking with Tile all this time? "Nevermind," he said, and walked out.

When Evan left, Tile poured herself a cup of tea, gently closed the door, and reached for her phone.

"Hello?" A man's calm and gentle voice spoke to Tile through the phone.

"Hello Gene, it's me. How are the girls?"

Evan had been doing his best to stay quiet and away from trouble since his talk with Professor Tile a week back. Classes focused on final exams for the semester before Christmas break, Cream was usually out of the room, and the only thing keeping Evan's hopes up was being able to see his family again over the holiday. Each day felt like a series of worries connected to each other, looping through his thoughts until he was too tired to think anymore. His MEBA read 37 by now, usually a score typical of a janitor or someone living on welfare. Evan felt like taking his MEBA into a government office to have it looked at for glitches might be too dangerous after Benny's disappearance; he could only pray that what was happening was a glitch that could later be restored properly so he could get a real job. He began to use his extra time, time that he used to pass talking to Benny, dreaming about what kind of job he could get. He had always wanted to work for large groups of people, doing things to improve their lives. While new inventions were fairly common, he didn't particularly want to hassle with all of the competition surrounding that field. Evan much rather wanted to find himself improving technology that already existed, and there were a lot of companies that needed people like that. It was a direction that seemed easy, safe, and profitable, if unexciting.

Tuesday night, before the final exams got underway, Evan had an especially difficult time sleeping. Cream had gone to bed long before, so Evan turned on the tv and put the subtitles on so as not to wake him. A news report came up about the harmful effects of grapefruit, but ended quickly. Just as Evan went to change the channel, the screen flipped over, showing the international news. The subtitles came up a few seconds after the broadcasters mouths moved, making his sleepy but worried brain try to link the two together. The subtitles read as follows:

"In international news, another anti-government event was halted due to the MEBA tracking of certain individuals. After the tragic loss of life seen previously in the area due to heart complications, military individuals were able to track and arrest a few of the members of the infamous Exodus group, stopping their supposed meeting at the King's Church in Cambridge. Among the arrested is Celeste Lewis, one of the highest ranking officers of Exodus. She is being taken to a secured location for questioning by Detective Robert Barnes, the hero responsible for finding the hidden secrets behind the Exodus member and close friend of Ms. Lewis, Amelia Rose. Although unwilling to comment at the time, Detective Barnes did say that he was excited about the opportunity to help bring peace into the area and end the threat of this powerful underground group. In local news…"

Evan flashed back to talking to Benny about the news, thinking of how he would interpret the story.

Benny would probably say "That's bogus." Evan imagined. "Why would they talk about how great this group is? They haven't done anything noteworthy that we know of."

"We don't know everything going on there." Evan responded in his own head, then adding "maybe they want to keep the negative stuff down since it's none of our business."

"If it's none of our business," Benny would have said, "then why put it as the only international news at night?"

Evan was stumped. Benny had somehow won the conversation against him without even being there. It made Evan realize how much he truly missed his friend. He fell asleep that night thinking of him and where he might be.

Another Professor Tile exam came and went and Evan, though he didn't realize it until it was too late, started tracking the answers in the back of his head to make sure he wasn't making any stupid mistake. He finished the test faster than he ever had before, turned it in and was almost positive he made a 100. He laughed at himself on the way back to his dorm room because he thought he was turning into Benny for a second. Pulling up his MEBA, it read 37 again. Maybe he had done enough to stop it from plummeting; maybe the diagnostics would be corrected after a malfunction. He stopped by his campus mailbox to check the mail in case they sent him anything. The only thing in there was a small note, written on college-ruled paper, sealed with a small piece of tape. Evan opened it as he walked, stopping to read it under one of the large oak trees on campus. It was from Jeremy:

Hey Evan,

My counselor had encouraged me to write more hand-written notes, so I figured I'd send one to you. Mom and Dad gave me your address. Thanks for being the best thing in my life. Mom and Dad may have raised me, but you made me awesome. Any luck on the corrupted file?

Love, Jeremy

It wasn't much, but Evan cried anyway. He always felt responsible for how Jeremy turned out and to see him being so genuine and thankful touched Evan's heart. He wiped the cold tears on his jacket and went back to his room. Cream wasn't there; no one was there. Evan didn't really have other people that he related to around him. His two closest friends were Benny and Professor Tile and Benny was gone. The loneliness of a campus without a best friend set in. His room seemed smaller, darker, and louder, even with no one around. He wanted to fill the vacant space in his brain, but wouldn't even know what to fill it with. Trying to drown out his negative emotions in reading didn't help much and he ended up soaking part of his pillow with tears. He wasn't aware of why he was even crying, but he couldn't stop. The more he cried, the more he wanted to cry. He lied to himself that it was just Jeremy's letter, but he couldn't find anything in his life otherwise that was going well enough to focus on and he was unable to admit to himself that his life seemed to be falling apart. His mind traveled from moment to moment, trying to piece things together, but being unable to do so. He only stopped because Cream had opened the door suddenly and the surprise of another noise startled him. Pulling himself together and waiting a while until he could fake happiness, Evan made his way to the kitchen to make dinner.

As Evan poured a can of soup into one of the two small pots they had, Cream came out of his room. "You look awful," he commented with a hint of compassion. "Are you okay?"

"No," Evan replied.

"Sorry man, anything I can help with?"

"No."

"Mind if I watch the news?"

"Yes." Evan thought for a second and changed his mind. "Go ahead. I'm just gonna eat in my room." When he went into his room the warm soup and exhausted mind caused him to fall right to sleep.

CHAPTER 3

The Blueprints

The drive home was hard. Since the radio in the car was busted, there was nothing to distract him from letting his brain come up with the worst possible situations. What if they destroy Benny's MEBA scores and force him to the lowest of the low? Would Benny be killed? Would they trace things back to him? What about his family? Can Professor Tile really be trusted? What if she is the reason Benny went missing to begin with? What was that device she started pulling out during their conversations? What if Cream is working with the government to keep tabs on me?

Evan ran over a few extra crunchy leaves that had piled up against the sidewalk in front of his family's home. The family car wasn't in the driveway. The large red brick building stood tall as a beacon of stability in his life. He had his first childhood kiss swinging on the bench on the porch and he had his first "real" kiss on the steps leading up to the porch. His high school friends would come by as a meeting spot and lounge around until someone came up with something important to do, or at least something so unimportant that it was interesting enough. Now the porch swing was gone, the wood slowly rotting away in a pile by the side of the house; the concrete steps had chunks taken out of them from dropping furniture being bought and brought in or sold and taken out; the bulb in the front room, old and dim from time, shone out on the cold day as the most insignificant source of light. The 20-year-old unlocked the door with the key he has had on his keychain for over a decade now and stepped into the entryway, shutting the door behind him.

"Hello," Evan called into the main hallway. "Hello?" He texted his family that he was headed home. The only noise to respond was a slight hum that he recognized as his old computer whirling away in his room. Jeremy probably had his headphones on and couldn't hear him. Plopping his back down at the foot of the stairs, he made his way up, avoiding the creaky step that he used to avoid when he was trying to hide the fact that he was getting home late. When he made his way to his old room, it was hard to think of it as "Jeremy's Room" still, only the computer greeted him with persistent humming. Stooping down, he motioned for it to come on and it did, greeting him with the ever welcoming dark blue background. Jeremy had about twelve windows opened at the same time, one thing that Evan and he never saw eye to eye on. He began closing them, but stopped about halfway through. On the computer screen flashed the corrupted file, but it was opened and no longer corrupted. Evan's mind darted around, trying to find a reason why or how, but he was too busy trying to answer the question of what to do with it.

"That's why everyone is gone," he spoke to himself. "Jeremy cracked open the file and the government came and took them all away." Muttering a bunch of "no's" under his breath, he started worrying about what to do with the file itself. Should he open its contents or just send it to himself? Should he show Tile? Is Jeremy part of all of this now?! Maybe he's part of the reason Benny went missing! Evan chuckled to himself at the thought. Something was finally so outrageous that it was impossible to worry about.

SLAM! The metal gate on the side of the house shook and rang its melody up to Evan's old room. After brushing off being startled, Evan went out to greet his family.

"Sorry we are late, honey," his mom apologized. "Christmas shopping." Behind her walked Jeremy and Roxie with what Evan had to assume was her boyfriend. He smiled and introduced himself as Slone; he seemed nice, Evan supposed, but maybe a little old for Roxie. Yeah, he was definitely too old for his little sister, Evan's protective brain went into overdrive. Before he could strike up anything more than awkward small talk, Jeremy rushed up and gave Evan a hug, whispering in his ear.

"I did it! Okay, well it wasn't just me that did it," the little brother explained while he hurried Evan upstairs to their room. "I brought the corrupted file to Mister Finnegan and he helped a lot. I told him that you did most of the work to get to the last passcode and he had a spare decoding drone laying about at the school that he used to hack in." Evan didn't want to mention that decoding drones were notorious for disseminating files without permission and that those that used them were often laughed at in college.

"Did you look at it?" Evan tried to pry without giving away his anxiety towards the file.

"Yeah," Jeremy didn't notice his older brother wincing. "It's all in a weird format though and I have no clue what it actually is yet. Maybe you can take a look." They sat down in the room, hunching over the computer as it sat on the carpeted floor Evan grew up on.

Before Evan could say anything else, Jeremy had opened the file without approval.

"It's a blueprint," Evan began describing.

"It's nothing like I've ever seen." Jeremy interrupted.

"Not surprising. It's a fairly complicated set of blueprints and it's not even a device I've seen before. It's coded all wrong. Whoever put this thing together has nearly everything backwards and upside down, not to mention out of order." Evan began moving things around as his personal cheerleader sat mouth half-open watching. "The separate parts of this thing are all organized by using an outdated system of stacking, a form of code that computers can't actually recognize because they never actually created an algorithm for breaking it down. It's a fairly elegant way to pass along information without anyone being able to intercept and decode it without someone being there who knows about this system of codes. Only person I've ever seen actually use it is…" He let out a long sigh, but wasn't sure if it was from relief of frustration. "Benny."

Because it was "stacked," it would take a couple of hours to undo unless Evan could figure out exactly how Benny had configured the packages that made up the blueprints. It would take some trial and error. Meanwhile, the call for dinner came up from downstairs.

"Common, Jer, let's work on this tomorrow. We will have more time then."

Dinner went by in a flash. The parents, always caring about their kids' futures, asked everyone about their MEBA scores.

32

"55," Roxie said. She had had a rough year and was caught cheating on a handful of tests, but had mostly made up the ground from her score dropping so much.

"72," Jeremy beamed.

"76," Evan lied. He figured that if his scores wasn't changing no matter what he did, he might as well use it to his advantage.

"81," Slone mentioned under his breath loud enough for the parents to hear.

"81!" Roxie's mom repeated loudly. "Well that is just wonderful. Tell me again what kind of things you like to do?" As so the conversation, much to Evan's delight, strayed into important but boring stories that highlighted Slone's work overseas during natural disasters. He did one out of necessity to fulfill community service hours for a college group he was a part of, but when he saw what it did to his MEBA score, he continued to do them.

"Doesn't hurt to pad the ol' score, eh?" Roxie's father chimed in and gave a glance over to her as though to say that she could always follow Slone on his next trip. She rolled her eyes.

"Well, as you know," the family patriarch steered the conversation, "we are going to be taking a trip down to Guatemala soon to scout out locations for the orphanage."

"Oh yeah," Evan thought to himself. "I really need to read the family email chains."

"We were thinking we can make our first trip out there just after new years. Jeremy wants to check it out and we can run a couple of scenarios by him that can help him keep up with his school work while we are out."

"Actually," it was unusual for Jeremy to speak out during meals, "I was thinking maybe I can stay here instead." A pregnant pause hung over the table for the briefest moment; Jeremy's voice got louder with the quiet and somewhat cramped room as he pitched his plan to everyone. "I can stay with James' family down the street and ride to school with him and Jillian is always nearby to keep an eye on me and I'm... that is...I guess I'm not really that excited about helping out in the orphanage."

"Oh," mother said, surprised but not hurt by Jeremy's sudden voice at the table. "You said a few weeks ago that you would love to come."

"Well, yeah, I guess. I think I might just miss home too much and be really bored there."

Father joined. "Thank you for letting us know. Let's talk about both options and you can pitch us your full plan in two days." Not exactly what Jeremy wanted to hear, but he was ready for it, nonetheless. "Pitching" an idea in the Roman household was a semi-regular occurrence and happened when someone wanted to do something that affected the family. The parents pitched the idea of the orphanage a few months ago (when Jeremy said he loved the idea), Evan had pitched changing his major a handful of times, and Roxie pitched a handful of decorative changes around the house. It was much less a way of deciding what to do as it was a way for the family to support "big ideas" and ask questions to help the presenter to make a good decision. Of the kids, only Jillian loved pitch meetings, but the others tolerated it enough since it was a family thing and it's really hard to get out of family things in the Roman household.

* * *

As they usually do when the house is full, Evan and Jeremy shared a room that night; Jeremy worked on his pitch on his phone while Evan began to work on the blueprint. For Evan, it was tough going at first; the order of the files did not follow typical standards for blueprints, but instead skipped around. The first file would have a piece and plan that needed an idea from the fourth file to work. Then it moved to the second file, back to the first, then the third, and by the time he put even one strand of the logic together, Jeremy was fast asleep, a near full presentation completed on the phone in his hands. Evan dimmed the lights with the room's remote and kept working.

The process of untangling the mess of files became easier as he worked, even to the point where Evan was able to guess which file was the next to complete the process more and more often, meaning he was backtracking less and compiling the blueprint order quickly. It wasn't until he was nearly finished that he noticed that the file order was repetitive; it always flowed from the first, then fourth, then second, first, third, fourth, and finally second. Then it would loop around. When he realized this, he created a quick algorithm that would decode the files himself and organize them properly. Running the algorithm through the files, the computer flashed the layers of files across the screen like a flipbook, but gave an error at the end of the process. The blueprint seemed to create a sort of chip, but Evan didn't know what it was used for or even where it would go. Oddly, it had halted the process with one file remaining. It was a hidden file that only appeared when all of the other files had been decoded and marked a sort of "endcap" to the blueprints. This is sometimes used to keep algorithms from completing their process and therefore requiring a real person rather than a computer to work the codes properly. None of this surprised Evan as he worked to complete his task, but the name of the file certainly caught him off guard: file 37.

* * *

Two hours of sleep wasn't really much to work with, but Evan managed to wake himself up properly with a cup of the only tea he could find in the house; it was bland and poorly balanced the mix of bitter and tart flavors that it claimed to have. Jeremy was already up, and began to barrage his older brother with questions before he was ready to say anything. Evan just ignored the onslaught.

"So what do you think it's for?" Jeremy continued to ask. Still no response. "Everyone else is gone, you have bags under your eyes, and you look like you are going to kill me. The only explanation is that you actually finished working last night. So what is it?"

"Shut up." Evan grumbled and immediately felt bad. He had never said that to Jeremy. He just couldn't take the continued prying. He knew that he wouldn't be able to keep everything from Jeremy for long. Either Jeremy's curious pestering or Evan's desire to include him in everything would give out and Jeremy would be a part of whatever Benny was wrapped up in. It didn't keep him from wanting to try to protect him for as long as possible. He added on to the distance he wanted to create with a "It was just a practical joke and I spent all night unpacking it for nothing. It was just a useless pile of code pretending to be something important."

Unsure whether to believe him or trust his gut that told him something was really off in Evan, Jeremy just replied with an "ok, fine" before leaving the room to go get ready for the day. Benny just sat there with his tea, starting into the cup, looking for something that would give him hope. After arguing with himself, he decided that he would contact Professor Tile. He sent her a couple of messages, asking if they could meet as soon as possible. They agreed to meet at a coffee shop halfway between the college and the Roman household.

"Hey Jer!" Evan called out. "I'm heading out to meet a buddy from college; be back later!"

"Fine, I've got things to do anyway," Jeremy's tone was bitter as he called down the stairs. As soon as the front door closed, he turned to the computer and began snooping through the code to find out if his brother was actually hiding something from him or not.

* * *

In the light of the mid-morning sun, Professor Tile's grey hairs began to shone brighter than ever as she sat and sipped her tea. She had already bought one for Evan when he arrived and found her sitting in the corner booth of "Cozy's Tea House". The student thought that his teacher looked a bit tired and weary and immediately began to think that he shouldn't have made his messages to her sound so critical. At this point, however, it was too late and he sat down on a lumpy cushion, wishing for the comfort of Tile's office. As she had done when they met in her office, the professor pulled out the little black device and tapped on it until the little green lights glowed.

"You have to tell me what that is," Evan demanded as much as one can to a teacher.

"I do not," she snapped back. Seeing the scared look on her student's face, she softened her tone after. "You seem troubled. What's going on?"

"Benny sent me something, and I think he wants you to know about it."

"What do you mean?"

"My little brother Jeremy was going through my high school files a few weeks ago and came across a corrupted file that he couldn't open. It took the help of one of his teachers, but he eventually cracked the password and inside of it was a set of blueprints. I spent most of last night putting them together. At first, I thought it was poorly written; everything was jumbled together, layered in weird ways, and it made the schematics difficult to even read. But then I noticed that there was a pattern, one that you might recognize." Evan pulled out one of Professor Tile's tests that he brought with him, highlighting the answers and writing them in a list together on the side of the paper, the number 37 at the end of it.

"Ah, haha," she had a good laugh. "I should probably explain something." She pushed another button on her device and another light came on. "Whether we like it or not, the world has decided that the best way to judge character is to use this MEBA system, right?" She began drawing out doodles on her paper; circles, lines, curves and the occasional word to go along with her speech. "This MEBA system, however, has a huge difficulty in it."

"Tile!" Evan called out quickly. "You shouldn't say things like that. If someone from the AMA really is tracking me down, you…"

Tile tapped on the device glowing green. "I have it covered and have since we started meeting." She leaned in a little bit. "It's the truth, Evan. MEBAs are good tools and some people use it to truly help keep them on the right track, like Roxie (whom Evan had discussed in detail during one of their long discussions). However, there is one thing that the MEBA system cannot accurately monitor. It tells you when you do something that feels right or makes you feel guilty, but it stops there. Think of it this way: you used to struggle in my classroom, making grades you didn't like and not fully understanding the material, right? It was a negative thing in your life. However, you chose to come and talk to me about it. I didn't change the mistake you had made, but you began to learn from me, understand how everything operates together, and you grew in your knowledge. Now that you know, for example, that quantifiable mechanisms in a biological environment, though they should not count towards the ideas of organisms in tribes, have begun being counted by those working with them as a means of determining population in semi-organic materials. It was a question that you missed on my first test, but now you understand those ideas and you use them all the time as we continue to learn. The MEBA system doesn't recognize when something has changed. It just takes and records information. Once information is a part of the system, it cannot be altered."

"Unless someone learns how to operate a backdoor and change their score without being detected by the system," Evan finished her idea.

"Exactly. But that is only the idea. Expand that to how the whole world uses the system. The world uses the system kind of like a scale, where things we do tip the scale one way or another. Benny didn't end up putting a giant weight on one side of the scale, he cut the chain that was holding the scale together. He wasn't after a way to tip the scale in his favor or to make himself look good in the eyes of others. He recognized that as long as the MEBA system is in place, someone can be 'perfect' and still be absolutely miserable."

Evan's face dropped. He couldn't help but think of all of he and Benny's conversations about other people and whether or not they deserved their scores and all of the comments he made about trying to get his score higher. Evan has made his score so important that it was more than just a number to him; it was an answer to how well he was doing in life. Benny's indifference wasn't a lack of care, it was a completely different way to look at the life.

"Professor," Evan snapped back into the conversation. "What will happen if Benny succeeds in what he is trying to do?"

"I think he already has," she looked straight at Evan. "Benny and I had many conversations that you never knew about, and Benny wanted to keep it that way. He talked about how since you were friends, you would make every decision based on how it would affect how you look to others. He said you were consumed with it; it was the only thing that drove you to success. In his thoughts, however, you were always successful because he enjoyed being around you. He cared more about you than you did, and he wanted to make this backdoor primarily so that you would stop putting so much of your life, your thoughts, and your time into making some automated system think you are doing well in life. He made this blueprint for you, not for him."

Could this be true? Evan took a deep breath. If it was true, why would Benny go through all of this trouble just for him? What if he didn't like what Benny was doing and just chose not to go along with it? Why didn't Benny even ask Evan if this is what he wanted?

Wouldn't all of this just have been easier if Benny and he had just done well in life and raised their MEBA scores together?

"Professor," Evan finally squeaked out amid his thoughts. "You said you talked to him a lot, right? Did he ever tell you why he wanted to do this?"

"He spoke of it constantly." Tile leaned back and sipped her tea. "How much time do you suppose you spent each day worrying about what you had or had not done?"

"Too much."

"How much did you care when other people were praised for their accomplishments or rejected for their failures?"

"Why does that matter?" Evan became a little offended. How much had Benny told Tile about their personal conversations?

"Did you ever miss out on spending time with Benny because you were worried about if something was right or wrong?"

"A few times."

"What do you think meant more to Benny: having a good MEBA score, or connecting with his best friend?"

A long pause drew out in the cafe. Outside the tall windows next to their booth, cars pulled in and out and people began making their way in for drinks.

"Evan, you are incredibly important; I see it. Benny has known it all along. You are a great person, but it isn't because of your score. He just likes you for you. You were enough of a reason for Benny to go through all of this mess." She paused for a second. "And it is certainly a mess isn't it?" They both chuckled a little bit. "What do you think you will do now that you know Benny's big idea?"

Another thought hit Evan, this one wasn't nearly as emotional, but it did feel more impactful, as though he finally realized what Benny was planning on doing.

"Professor," he said calmly for the first time in this conversation. "I think Benny got caught on purpose. Think about it. He's too smart to get caught because of some silly error and he now knows how to go about undetected by the MEBA system. What good does it do him to turn himself in to the authorities?"

"I honestly don't know. He never told me. Knowing Benny, he probably has a reason."

* * *

After his conversation with Professor Tile, Evan headed back to his home, fully ready to apologize to Jeremy for treating him so poorly that morning. He rehearsed his apology in his head many times; after the third time, he realized that he should take Jeremy to get some ice cream when they had finished. It got to the point where he felt like he had already apologized and was just ready to have some fun with his little brother. However, when he pulled around the corner onto his street, he slammed on his breaks instead.

Three cars, marked with the AMA's seal, were parked in front of his home. Two well dressed men stood upright next to the car. Evan's heart began pounding. Chills ran up and down the back of his neck. He could see the door to his home being pulled open from the inside. Like a procession at a funeral, out walked 4 more well dressed men, each carrying some of Jeremy's computer equipment and one of them, in the back of the group, with his hand on Jeremy himself. The man pushing along Jeremy was tall and narrow, his black hair coiffed rigidly to the left side of his head. He was holding a small book that from a distance seemed like a journal of sorts. When he stopped and pulled out the gold lined pen from his pocket to write in the book, the others carrying the computers stopped as well, as if they were linked together by invisible rope. Moments passed as the narrow man wrote and his lips moved. Evan could see Jeremy talking a little as well, which only made Evan cringe thinking of what Jeremy must be telling them. The small black book was closed and the gold-lined pen returned to the pocket from which it was pulled and the narrow man restarted the march to the cars. They all walked single file and loaded up the computer equipment into the vehicle, with the young high schooler who was clearly responsible for possessing the technology the last to be put in the car. The door was opened to him and Jeremy ducked into the car.

"Benny didn't plan for this," Evan blamed his best friend under his breath. Whether from fear or self-preservation, he could not seem to move save pulling the car to the side to get out of the way of the vehicles. They slowly started their cars, slowly pulled out from in front of Evan's house, and slowly drove down the street. Evan quickly hid under his steering wheel so as not to be seen, although for some reason he was more worried to be seen by Jeremy than the well-dressed men. One deep breath, then two, then five and finally Evan had the courage to look and see that no one was there any longer. No one was guarding the house or waiting for him to come back. As he looked down, Evan knew it was just him and his score of 37 to keep him company.

CHAPTER 4

Underground

"Evan, can you and Jeremy come set the table?" the call from mom echoed through the old home. It had been two hours since Evan lied and told his parents that he and Jeremy were working on Jeremy's big school project.

Three hours ago, Evan had started to plan. His train of thought trailed into a set of logical steps that he rehearsed in his brain until he actually believed all of them. The officials in charge of the MEBA system had taken Benny and Jeremy, the former because what he created, and the latter because they think he is a part of what was created. If both of them were a part of this process, then they likely would be taken to the same place. Evan couldn't bear to think that they were both there because of him. He began to blame himself for whatever was going to happen to them.

So Evan set into motion his own connection to the device that Benny created. If his two best friends were taken in, he might as well be also. He didn't have Jeremy's computer on which to send out information on the technology and he didn't want his parents to potentially be linked into this childish plan, so he drove back to Delvedale to use his personal computer. He sent a handful of messages: a couple to his family, telling them that he and Jeremy were going to go out to eat to celebrate "a job well done", and one to Professor Tile that simply stated that he wanted to find "where this 37 thing really leads." She should be able to piece it together, he thought as he sent it. Finally, he sent out an email to Benny and to Jeremy saying that he had "unlocked the potential of the device and was now off the MEBA system" and that "no one would be able to track him from now on."

Cheesy, Evan thought. But they can't ignore such an obvious connection.

An hour passed. Evan began to question his decision. He paced in his room, talking to himself the entire time. What if Benny didn't want him to be caught? What if he just ruined everything. What would he even say to Benny if he was there? What if they don't take me to the same place?

A gentle knock on the door interrupted his focused worrying.

"Who is it?" Evan questioned, grabbing his backpack, computer, and MEBA.

"Mr. Roman," a voice seemed to echo from the other side of the door. "We need to speak to you about some issues concerning your MEBA. Evan walked to the door, his heart beating wildly. Even though he knew this was going to happen, it still caused him to panic. "No turning back" he thought to himself and opened the door despite his sweaty palm greasing the metal knob.

Before him stood the tall and narrow man with the coiffed black hair. His eyes were dusty brown and everything about him seemed perfectly proper; his suit was neatly pressed and navy and the tie around his neck matched it perfectly. His hands were folded neatly against his body, somewhat rigid and cracked like a coal miner, but the fingernails were manicured and cleaned. His shoes were tied in such a way that the loops on them even seemed like they were the exact same distance apart from the knot in the middle. Evan expected there to be other people, but only the narrow man stood politely in the doorway, tilting his head ever so slightly so as to meet eyes with Evan.

"May I come in?" the narrow man offered his hand and spoke gently, his accent coming from somewhere Evan didn't recognize.

"Of course," the boy was a bit shocked by the start of the conversation. He was ready to be cuffed and forced out of his apartment. Instead, he found himself gesturing to the filthy couch that was laden with chip crumbs.

"Thank you very much," the man replied. Evan sat across from him in the chair. As he spoke, the narrow man often paused in the middle of his sentences, looking for the exact word he wanted to use. At first, it seemed that he might have some sort of speech impairment, but the more he talked, the more Evan thought it might just be how he talks. "My name is Jonathan Pierce. I represent the Agency of MEBA Affairs. We deal with all sorts of… accidental errors with the MEBA system and work with people to fix problems in the system itself. We believe that your roommate may have, unbeknownst to you, been tampering with your device. Have you noticed anything… unfamiliar with your MEBA or its scores recently?"

Evan gulped loudly. "Yes," he squeaked out. "It started dropping a while ago and then got stuck. I don't know anything that might have made it fall though." He knew he was kind of lying, but he also was telling the truth for the most part. Whether it triggered his score to move or not didn't really matter to him at this point.

"Have you ever... had something like this happen to your device before?"

"No, sir."

"Have you had any surgeries over the past year or so?"

"Never, sir."

"This roommate of yours, Benny; are you close?"

Evan couldn't figure out how to answer. If he said no, he may not have a chance to see him, but if he said yes, it could prove his guilt... if he was even guilty.

"Yeah, we are. I've known him since I started college. We lived together for three years now."

"Tell me a little bit... about your friend."

"He's a good guy. Really smart. Hates the news. Really opinionated." Evan scrambled for other things to say.

"Smart enough to get away with tampering with the MEBA system and not being caught?"

Wait, Evan thought to himself. Did Benny not get found out? Did he run away and actually stay off their radar? Am I going to get in trouble and not even be able to see or talk to Benny through all of this?

"The reason I ask," Mr. Pierce continued, "is because he came to us a couple of weeks ago telling us that he knew how to undo the system. He has... chosen not to show us this information just yet. We are holding him in our facility until he either... releases the information he claims to have or... we find out that he is simply pulling our legs. Since Benny is a friend of yours and you think he is… capable of creating something that… upsets the MEBA system, we feel that it may be beneficial for you to come with us and maybe… speak to Benny and see if you can get him to… pass along the information he has. We will only use that knowledge to ensure that hard working people like yourself receive a fair opportunity to do well and… raise your scores properly."

The way that Mr. Pierce spoke was simultaneously calming and frustrating. Evan couldn't help but feel that the gentleman was choosing his words in such a way that he was trying to manipulate Evan; at the same time, it was easy to trust his relaxed way of speaking and his consistent, reassuring tone.

"So what do you say, Mr. Roman? Would you be able to… assist us in this way?

Evan thought to himself that this was the only way that he could see Benny again, and now he at least knows that Benny really is with them and that he will be able to talk to him again.

"Yeah, I can help."

"Follow me please," Mr. Pierce asked nicely and gestured toward the door as he arose from the couch and continued to talk as they walked outside and down the apartment steps to the sleek car parked in Benny's parking spot. "For your safety, you should understand that we will need to borrow your MEBA so that we can properly fix it. We will also need to take a closer look at your computer and any other devices you may use on a regular basis to see if Benny has sent or communicated to you in any way that may help us to fix this problem we all have." One more well-dressed suit was waiting downstairs with the car and he opened the door for Evan and closed the door when Evan was seated safely in the vehicle.

A great deal of unease came over Benny's friend as the car started pulling away. He could not quite pin down where the feeling came from, but it grew stronger as they drove. Evan began to question all of the decisions he had previously made, both recently and, strangely enough, those he had made from his childhood as well. Small things that once seemed insignificant came back like haunting dreams that would return in the night, unwilling to leave until they have been stirred around in his head.

The ride was smooth and easy and the leather seats were surprisingly warm in the sunlight of what would otherwise be a cold and bitter day. Whether from stress or finally being able to relax, Evan found himself dreary and eventually he fell asleep leaning up against the door of the car.

After an hour or so, the sunlight streaming through the side window heated up Evan's face, causing him to stir and adjust. He moved slowly, aching from sleeping sideways without a cushion to support him. Out the window, a section of highway stretched forward, the rolling hills and deciduous trees giving him something to look at during the cold season. When staring out of the window became boring, Evan got to figuring out where exactly he was. This wasn't the way home to the south, so he must be heading north. A sign that read "HWY 501" hung crooked on the side of the road. Evan realized that he was further east than he expected, meaning that the car had taken them further away from cities and into the less populated countryside. A few miles later, as he started to think that sleeping may be a good idea again, he saw what looked like hikers standing on the side of the road, their car sitting by the side of the highway. It would not have been a bit interesting to Evan, but he recognized that the car on the side of the road looked similar to the one he was in; both had the AMA's logo on the side door. He focused for a closer look at the hikers as they approached. One of them, appearing to be a male with a hoodie and jeans on, seemed to be badly hurt, holding on to the taller gentleman, lanky and long. The appearance of the taller gentleman reminded Evan of Mr. Pierce with a slight slouch. Before he could get a good look though, the car whizzed by, even speeding up a little bit as they passed. As much as Evan wanted to stay awake, his eyelids, heavy in the afternoon sun, lulled him into another backseat sleep.

* * *

The jolt from crossing a speedbump woke Evan Roman and he began to take in his surroundings. Out of the tinted window, a large building stood wide, the blocky structure telling that it had aged a few decades. The walls were browned brick-like stones, some of them extending to each other supported by pillars instead of walls, like the colonnade of long-forgotten civilizations. The door to the polished car was opened for him and the bright sun beat against his eyes, contrasting the cold air that blew his jacket open. The air was thick with a wretched smell that he could only assume was garbage baking in the mid-winter sun. Based on the uneven texture of the parking lot, Evan was surprised that the rocky gravel didn't wake him before the speedbump.

"This way please," the narrow man gestured for Evan to get out. On the arch of the building, Evan read the words "Hendrose High School."

"A high school?" he questioned, assuming that something had gone wrong.

"We work for… many nations, some of which do not really like what we do. We take precautions to… ensure the safety of our employees."

"How would the headquarters of a major corporation be here though?"

"Headquarters? No, this is just a satellite campus that is used to… monitor and protect the local area." Mr. Pierce replied. "It's not the most… convenient place but it works for what we need."

After providing a passcode on the outer door's security system, Mr. Pierce opened the door to the building, the lights above shone from the high ceilings, but were dulled by all of the brown stone on the wall. The tall, thin man wove his way down two hallways filled with doors that were most likely old school rooms. Each door was covered over so that Evan couldn't see inside, despite his desire to do so. Considering himself a bit of a spy, he wanted to gather as much information as he could. Behind Evan walked the well-dressed man who drove them here. There seemed to be no other evidence of people, much less an entire organization dedicated to monitoring potential threats against a system that everyone in the civilized world uses. Evan had a difficult time thinking that the AMA would actually be able to operate here; the place seemed completely empty, no technology, no people, no activity.

Down at the end of the darkened hallway, one door, with white door frame panels and a hand scanner, stood out like a sore thumb from the rest of the dreary hallway. Mr. Pierce put his hand up to the scanner, which emitted no additional light, but gave a click after a couple of seconds. He then opened the door and ushered Evan into the room, which the boy was surprised to find was actually an elevator. He quickly scanned the buttons to get an idea of how big this place was. Was it a huge underground basement that extended for endless hallways? The three buttons on the elevator told a different story than Evan was imagining. The buttons read "0", "B1", and "B2". Mr. Pierce pushed "B1" and the door slowly shut and only reopened when the elevator had descended to the floor below.

Evan couldn't help but see Mr. Pierce in the entire layout and organization of the floor to which the door opened; everything was perfectly neat, perfectly placed, and perfectly tidy. The room was large, Evan suspected about 100 yards or so stretched before him; the ceiling stood high overhead, at least forty or so feet, the fluorescent lights giving a faded blue tint to the white paint. When the elevator opened with a bell's ding, the expanse of the first "basement" floor wouldn't give the slightest noise back. It was almost as though no one worked here. However, there were guards lining the main hallway every thirty or so feet, silent and staring straight ahead, their arms on their sides. The guards were dressed professionally, all in suits of various colors, and all of those suits well pressed and well fitted. On the right side of the long, wide hallway were five white doors with white handles and white hinges. None of the doors had any sort of markings on them, but each had a guard standing near them, blinking only when necessary.

On the left hand side of the hallway, were five large, enclosed rooms, the walls made of some sort of thick plexiglass, enabling people to see the entirety of what was going on inside. Each room was set up similarly to a hotel room with a comfortable looking bed, a desk, lamp, computer, a bookshelf, and a swivel chair. In the first room, all of the furniture was a light, dusty blue color. The second room was red, the third was green, the fourth dusty purple, and the last room was black. They were the only bits of color in the otherwise white-washed hall. Evan tilted his head to see that there seemed to be a lump in the bed of the final, black room near the end of the hallway. He didn't feel comfortable asking Mr. Pierce who it was, although he was hoping that it was Benny or Jeremy.

Down at the end of the hallway, Evan spotted a desk with a white computer about three or four times the size of his computer and a white chair perfectly facing the exact center of the desk. From behind the desk, an individual with a similar suit to Mr. Pierce stood up, adjusted his chair to face the center of his desk again, and walked calmly down the hall. Before Evan stood a man taller than Mr. Pierce but his board shoulders and square face made his height seem much less important. He also had a navy suit on, nicely pressed and looking brand new. His blocky chin did its best to distract from his larger-than normal ears, which hung awkwardly on the sides of his face. Extending his hand, the large, blocky man introduced himself.

"Greetings, Mr. Roman," his voice was strong, thick, and stern. Evan couldn't help but think from his almost raspy voice that hospitality may not be his greatest strength. "Thank you for coming here with us to fix this situation." Each word came out like it was rehearsed from a script a thousand times and no longer had any meaning.

"My name is Mr. Crib. I am the manager of this facility. Please, let me show you around." Then turning to Mr. Pierce and the driver, Mr. Crib added "Would you mind fetching Mr. Roman's things and bringing them in for inspection?" There was an odd way that Mr. Crib would speak, soft and calm at the start of the sentence but rising up in volume and intensity in the middle before trailing off at the end. Evan thought he may have some speech disorder, but he certainly wasn't going to mention it. The youth instantly missed the odd dialect and long pauses of Mr. Pierce as he was passed from one navy suit to the next. Mr. Crib waited for Mr. Pierce and the driver to get back onto the elevator before he turned back to his new guest.

"So, you are a bright boy, I am told. I'm sure you have questions that you would like to ask. Please understand that this is a place where all of your questions can be answered. I will happily pass along any information that I can to comfort your mind. Now, how may I serve you?"

It was strange that Mr. Crib asked this question, which also seemed unusually rehearsed. It was even stranger that Evan didn't really seem to be able to think of any questions off the top of his head.

"I think a tour would be fine," Evan heard himself say as he stared at the room with the black furniture, hoping to get close enough to see if his friend or his brother were being kept there.

"Very well then," Mr. Crib smiled without his voice perking up at all. "What would you like to know?"

"I don't know," Evan, feeling like he needed to talk properly, overemphasized the "t" in "don't" and the "n" in "know". He tried to think of an interesting question, but only came up with: "How many people work here?"

"Twelve," Mr. Crib responded.

"What?" Evan exclaimed, emphasizing nothing. "This place is huge. How can you run it with only twelve people?"

Mr. Crib slowly began to walk down the hallway towards his desk as he answered Evan's question. "Well you see, most of the system is of course data and computers. Through each of these doors are a bunch of computers that help to make sure the system stays regulated."

"Stays regulated?"

"Of course. MEBAs are only able to measure the physical reactions from guilt that the body tells it to. There are people in the world without your moral compass that actually believe that some things are okay when they clearly are not. For example, most people would barely have cared about the little lies that you told your family and your brother; they would have said that it was okay to lie to them because it was protecting those that they love and protection is more important than truth. We recognized immediately that you knew it was a lie and so it was categorized as such. In order to make sure that the system is properly gathering information, it needs to make constant adjustments to what people think is right in order to make sure it is calculating each decision properly and not weighing the choice based on if someone actually thinks they are doing the correct thing. It wouldn't be a successful system if the world was able to determine what was right or wrong based on its narrow thinking."

"That makes sense," Evan nodded gently. And it did make sense. Everything that Mr. Crib mentioned was actually very logical and helped people a lot.

The stern, thick voice continued as they walked down the long, wide hallway. "Behind this door is the part of the system that sends out the data to all of the MEBAs located nearby and updates their scores, think of it like a large indoor satellite that pushes out all of the relevant information we gather here." He motioned to the door as they passed; then he gestured to those standing near them as he spoke. "The guards that you see standing here are vital to our success as well. Each of them is highly paid and skilled at their jobs." Evan couldn't help but think of a sarcastic remark about how easy it is to be skilled at standing around looking bored. He was surprised when Mr. Crib stopped and shook the hand of the guard they were standing next to.

"How is your family Mr. Garrett?"

The man returned the handshake, looked his supervisor directly in the eye and responded in a tone similar to Mr. Crib's. "They are very well thank you."

"Your daughter's ballet recital is coming up isn't it?"

"It is this upcoming Friday."

"I will make sure that I am there; I know that she has been trying very hard and having support from all of us will help her do her very best I am certain."

"Thank you sir. We will make sure to save you a seat."

Mr. Crib put a hand on the guard's shoulder and turned to Evan. "I believe this spring will mark Mr. Garrett's fourth year with us. He is a fine and upstanding man and he deserves recognition for his work."

He walked on and had a similar conversation with each of the four remaining guards, to one he mentioned a sick family member and what the group could do to support them financially, and to two others he greeted them jovially and proceeded with small talk for about a minute. Each conversation was unique, but Even still felt that what he was saying had been rehearsed previously. It was as though Mr. Crib had been trained in such a way to carry on perfectly meaningful conversations and did so well at it that the conversations no longer seemed to have meaning.

Evan stopped listening during the third conversation as they managed to make it halfway down the hall. While Mr. Crib talked to the third guard, Evan finally got a glimpse of the person in the room with the black furniture. It was a man laying down on top of the silky, shiny black seats; however, it wasn't Benny or Jeremy. All that Evan could make out was a mop of black hair and a body that seemed average in all ways. In the room was also a set of books lined neatly on a bookshelf and a clipboard that hung on the handle of the see-through door, facing the inside of the room. When Evan finally snapped back and gave his attention to the "tour" he was receiving, they were already at the last guard at the last door, meaning he had missed an entire conversation and a half while his mind wandered off to the man in the black room.

"Hello Mr. Jones. How are you doing today?" Mr. Crib started the conversation like all of the others.

"I'm good thank you," the guard spoke softly and gently, but looked uncomfortable while he did. He seemed somehow different to Evan than the other guards. While the others seemed like Mr. Crib was having a polite conversation with a mirror, this guard felt a bit more normal, like an employee talking to his boss.

"How is your wife doing?"

"She is good," Jones responded.

"Is she enjoying her new job?"

"I think so. She doesn't say much about it."

"I hope it goes well for her. Starting a new career can be stressful but very enjoyable."

"Thank you sir." Jones went to try to end the conversation with a handshake.

"Have a good day." Mr. Crib returned the handshake.

Evan just stood there, watching the entire boring conversation like a little kid watching his parents talk to their friends. He stayed quiet; when Mr. Crib began walking again, he followed behind him, giving one final glance to the last guard as he went. He had been keeping in mind the number of people he had come across, counting eight in his head when they finished with the guards. There was one unmarked door near Mr. Crib's perfectly positioned desk that had no guard at it. Evan motioned to it and asked what it was for.

"Those are the stairs," Mr. Crib stated blankly. "They lead down to the next floor.

"What other things need to get done in order for the organization to run?" He asked, trying to figure out as much as he could about where Benny or Jeremy might be.

"We have a records room, where we keep any important files related to those that we are watching, just in case something happens with the MEBAs system. There is a gentleman who has been with the AMA for over twenty years that words there to keep the records in perfect order. We also have someone who is here to try to improve the system itself, sort of a research and development role."

Evan counted nine employees if the driver was one of them and only eight if he wasn't. "In what ways can the system be improved?" He dug deeper in his questions, hoping to find the last few employees.

"We have not found any just yet, but we are hoping that someone can still assist us in perfecting the technology. We are always looking for the best and the brightest minds to make us operate more smoothly."

Evan couldn't help but think of Benny, and remembered that the only reason Mr. Pierce brought him here was to talk to Benny. "Where is Benny?" He surprised himself when he asked, and then rephrased the question, quickly going back to overemphasizing his words. "I mean to say that you brought me here to try to talk Benny into figuring out what he may or may not have done to my MEBA. If you still want me to talk to him, when would I be able to do that?" As his tongue tripped over half of his words, Evan had difficulty not sounding desperate in his voice.

Mr. Crib's seemingly forced smile turned to a blank expression. "He is resting right now after refusing to talk last night. He stayed up all night long just staring at the wall. We are becoming concerned for his well being. Let's get you situated and comfortable first so that he feels safe talking to you. You need to convince him that everything here is fine and that he needs to stop trying to undo the hard work this company and its employees have done." Mr. Crib walked Evan down the long, wide hallway back the way they came, past the shaggy-haired man in the black furniture room, past the five guards and the five doors. Evan wanted more than anything to ask where Benny was, but couldn't muster the courage to do so. He thought that Mr. Crib liked him and knew it would be more likely to get what he wanted if he didn't ruffle any feathers.

Mr. Crib led Evan up to the first clear, plexiglass room, the one with the light blue furniture. On the outside of the door was a small scanner that Mr. Crib put his finger to to open the door. "For your safety." He said as he opened the locked room. "If you need anything at all, put it on this form please," he motioned to the computerized clipboard hanging in the middle of the door and then proceeded to point out Evan's computer, phone, and a few sets of clothes from his home. "As you can see, we have already put your personal belongings here to help you feel at home. Since you are here to assist us in our jobs, please know that we are here to make sure every need of yours is met to the highest standards. All food will be provided for you, any specific needs for reading material, technical help with your computer, and any other thing you can think of will be provided for you. In addition, you may adjust the walls so that you can keep others from seeing inside." He tapped lightly on the plexiglass next to the door, which brought up a set of options for the walls and lighting of the room. "This is primarily used for nighttime so that you can sleep peacefully, but can also be adjusted for low-light. We will never interrupt you if you wish to be left alone. If there is something we need from you or we are about to bring something to you, a small light will flicker so that you can know we are coming to greet you. If you need a moment to adjust your personal appearance, you just push this button here, and it will give you two minutes to get ready. The guard across the hall from you will protect you from any harm."

"Harm?" Evan realized that it seemed out of place.

"Sadly, the world does not guarantee safety, so we guarantee it for you. One less thing to worry about, right?" the blocky face tried its best to smile, but only managed to slightly spook Evan with its forced grin.

After the tour and his new personal room, Evan could only ask himself how long Mr. Crib thought this would take. Evan imagined that it would only be a few hours at most, a quick conversation with Benny, find Jeremy, and go home. Instead, it felt like he was being invited to stay in a hotel room for an indefinite amount of time.

"Do you know where my brother Jeremy is? He mentioned working on something and I thought I saw one of your cars at our house recently." Evan didn't want to overstep the information he had, but hadn't heard anything related to his brother and his brain was getting itchy from the lack of answers he was receiving from Mr. Crib.

"Jeremy?" the thick voice questioned before a quick answer showed across his face. "Ah yes, the fellow that was in here yesterday. Nice boy. Good student from what I've heard. Mr. Pierce spoke to him mostly; it seemed as though you and he had shared some devices and Mr. Pierce thought that he might have been the one connected to Benny. We sent him home with the best regards. Do you want us to go get him? Did you need to speak to him?"

Evan wasn't sure, so he said that he didn't; knowing that Jeremy was safe at home was enough for now.

"Well let me know if you change your mind. If you put it on that clipboard, we will surely be able to help you out. Just so you know, the door will lock behind you and will only open from this side. This is to ensure your safety. We are happy to open the door for you whenever you need."

Evan's heart sank deep into his chest. This was the first time that he suddenly felt completely powerless, as though he had been tricked and all of his choices were taken away from him. In his mind, it was clear that he wasn't being manipulated; Mr. Crib and Mr. Pierce were always up front with him and both were men of their words. However, something deeper inside of him began to scream out as though trying to catch him before he made a mistake.

Mr. Crib politely closed the door behind him with a click and the door lock slid itself into place.

CHAPTER 5

Conversations

The rest of the day passed slowly. Through the clipboard, Evan asked for some pizza, which came in about 10 minutes, piping hot and delicious. He devoured the whole thing as he tried to decide what to do with his time. Using the computer felt a little worthless; who would he communicate with and what would he say? Certainly the association that invited him in would be monitoring everything he did. He thought over and over again about sending a message to his brother, asking if he actually came here and what Mr. Pierce spoke with him about, but that too seemed a bit risky. He ended up reading his microbiology textbook that the company brought from his home for him. As he flipped through, he looked for any random words that were highlighted, cut out, or tampered with in any other way. Maybe, he considered, Benny had already known this was going to happen and he left him some kind of clue in his stuff like he did with the blueprints. The blueprints! If the group took his computer, they would be able to look into the blueprints and find that Evan really did know what was going on. This was bad. Really bad. What Evan wouldn't give for a cup of tea and a conversation with Professor Tile right now. Sitting there, he realized that he might just be able to do that.

On the clipboard, he wrote down that he wanted a tutor from his college for his microbiology and tech class and some of the tea that he knew she always made for him. The guard who stood across the hallway guarding the first door came up to read the board, took the piece of paper from it, went down to Mr. Crib and showed it to him. Evan began to sweat and his heart began to beat loudly as he watched the guard slowly make his way back to the door.

The guard spoke gently. "We will be contacting an instructor at your school to come and tutor you. There is an expert in microbiology and tech there named Ms. Tile. She should be able to assist you in your work."

"Thank you," Evan squeaked out sheepishly.

And so he read and waited. Exhaustion took over, the pizza made its way into his digestive system, and Evan fell asleep waiting and hoping.

* * *

It was dark when he woke up, the entire hallway enveloped in stillness. The only lights were a set of dim red lights that flickered on and off above the doors that the guards stood by. Evan didn't remember seeing those lights during his "tour" of the facilities. His vision felt fuzzy, as if looking through a half-torn quilt with patches missing and pieces fading away. In the grogginess of waking up quickly, there were too many changes to take in all at once. Not only the lights, but the entire place felt different. It felt… more hopeful, more peaceful, more exciting even. Suddenly, Evan's head began to ache, throbbing to the point where he felt the need to hold the pain inside as much as he could by clenching his head with both of his hands.

He glanced around for the clipboard to write on, but in the pain and confusion, he only found the hook that usually held it in place. Glancing down, the clipboard was broken in half, the paper, the pen, all of it. Perfectly cut all the way through, leaving no stray edges or bits of wood lying around. That's when he noticed a pair of over-worn, faded, fraying sneakers standing in the doorway.

It couldn't be…

"Benny!" Evan jumped up and gave his best friend a hug. As he did, the pain in his head started pounding again, causing him to whence in pain. Evan pulled Benny from the doorway somewhat forcefully into his room and began to whisper, trying to ignore the pounding. "What is going on?"

"I'm busting you out," Benny said in a voice far too normal for the situation.

"What do you mean? I'm not a prisoner here. I came to talk to you!"

"Ok," Benny's tone stayed completely calm. "What do you want to talk about?"

"Everything! The device you made got you taken away and I came to follow you because I thought you needed me to bust you out and I cracked the code on your blueprints which lead to this cool looking microchip that you made, but by that time they already had you and they took Jeremy too for a while but they seem to have him back now…"

"Slow down," Benny put his hand on his friend's shoulder. Evan looked him in the eyes for the first time, only to find a mountain of bruises, scratches and scars on his discolored, puffy cheeks.

"Benny, your face. What happened?"

"Oh, right. They beat me up."

"Why?"

"That's a long story. I'll tell you the whole thing later."

"Did you end up destroying the MEBA system?"

"What do you think?" Benny said sarcastically enough to get the point across to Evan. "So are you ready to get out of here Evan?"

"Sure. Let me just get my stuff."

"What stuff?" Benny asked.

Evan turned around and sure enough his things weren't in the room. His computer, his MEBA, his clothes. Everything had vanished.

"Come on," Benny began to speak more hurriedly.

Evan stood up, still in pain, still confused and still having a hard time seeing. Benny led him out of his room and into a group of people, four others standing there as though they were waiting for him to come out. For some reason, perhaps out of upbringing, he shook each person's hand and introduced himself as politely as he could.

The first person shook his hand back. Her handshake was unusually dainty, like that of royalty addressing their people. When he went to look at her, his vision blurred again, but he caught brown eyes, a rounded chin, and long dirty blonde hair.

The second person, when his vision focused enough, was actually two people who looked the same. Instead of shaking hands, they simply placed their hands around his as though to comfort him.

By the touch of their cold but gentle hands, Even imagined that both of them were girls. They stood about the same height, a little taller than Evan and their voices were very different, although even as it was happening, he couldn't actually hear the words they were saying, only how they were saying it. One voice he felt was direct and calm like Benny's was while the other voice sounded more upbeat and melodic.

The third person was a man, dressed nicely and standing straight-backed. His voice and his handshake were friendly. "It is very nice to have you here with us." Evan heard him say, realizing that the others probably spoke as well, but in his confusion and pain, he forgot what they said.

Benny began to lead the group down the long hallway towards Mr. Crib's desk. "The elevator is shut down for now. We will have to go this way."

Evan followed behind everyone else, making decisions seconds after the others seemed to. From the back of the line, he could see the guards, all either asleep or…. Maybe dead? The four other rooms were all empty still, except the last room, the one with the black furniture. The shaggy-haired man stood upright in the last room and for some reason Evan could see every detail about him. His hair actually came down to the top of his shoulders. He was dressed in a gray button-up shirt and slacks, nice tan shoes to match his tan belt, and light blue eyes. Evan made a quick judgement on him that he seemed very nice. His hands were gently placed in his pockets and his head tilted slightly as he watched the group make their way down the hallway.

"Wait! Benny!" The group stopped when Evan called out. "What about him?"

Benny gave no response that Evan could see, only started walking again, past the final door, this one with no guard standing watch over the black room like usual. The group followed Benny as he led them into the last door in the hallway, the door that Evan remembered led to the downstairs document room. Benny stood at the door, holding it open for the others to walk in and start heading to the spiralled stairs that led up, likely to the outside of the building. When Evan got up to Benny, he stopped.

"Benny, who are all of these people? What's up with that guy in the black room? Are the guards dead? Tell me what's going on!"

Benny looked Evan straight in the eyes. He looked excited and also really sad.

"I've been looking forward to this for a long time. I knew you would make the right choice. You had the key in you the entire time. Do your part well and we will celebrate when we are all done." The room began shifting in Evan's head and he felt himself pulled out of the experience of walking, talking, seeing things. He recognized the feeling and realized he was waking up, but did not want to. He tried willing himself there, predicting what would happen next. He tried walking into the room that led downstairs, but it only caused him to pull further out of the dream in his head.

* * *

Evan woke up in a cold sweat, trying to catch breath that he already had. He surveyed his room as quickly as he could: his computer, clothes, and books were all there. It was odd being in a place where other people watched you wake up; it felt intrusive in the most personal way. Even so, the guard on the other side of the hallway stared straight ahead, possibly watching, possibly daydreaming. As Evan put his feet to the floor and shook off the covers that still clung to his legs, the guard opposite him began to walk over to his room. Evan slipped on his jeans over his boxers as quickly as he could and found a shirt he hadn't worn yet to put on.

"Mr. Roman," the guard spoke when Evan was finishing getting dressed. "We have brought in a tutor to assist you while you are here. Please let me know when it is good for you to have her come in."

Moments later, after Evan had tidied up his room, he requested for them to bring the tutor in, hoping that it was actually Professor Tile. When she stepped in, he was elated and realized that he needed to make her some tea for it to be a "proper" meeting. When the guard let her in the door, he asked that he make some of the tea he had sent for.

"You will have to put your request in writing," the guard responded robotically. Evan hurriedly put down what he wanted and handed it to the guard. "I'll be happy to meet your request Mr. Roman."

The see-through door closed and the lock slid into place with a whirring sound. Evan didn't really know how to host a meeting like this, especially with others looking around, so he pulled out a chair for his teacher and sat on his unmade bed.

"Hello there," Professor Tile said cautiously. It was good to hear her British accent again. She reached for her pocket and began pulling out the device with the green lights.

"I don't know if that thing will work here," Evan warned. "I'm pretty sure this entire place is bugged."

She clicked it anyway, put it back in her pocket, and smiled. "It will work." A pause hung in the air, like old friends waiting for the other to start a conversation after not having seen each other for years. "So how are you?" Tile finally asked.

"I'm okay I think. This place is really weird"

"I've been waiting outside for 3 hours."

"Sorry about that. I was having a weird dream."

"You keep saying weird. What is weird?"

Evan thought for a few moments. "I don't really know. It's not what I expected, but this place doesn't seem evil or corrupt or anything like that. Everyone is really nice and works hard and is good at what they do. I imagine this is what working at a place you enjoy is like. But…"

Professor Tile sat staring and folding her thin hands, waiting for him to finish his sentence.

"Something just feels… off." Evan leaned back against the clear wall his bed was next to; on the other side was the second room with the red furniture. "Do you think I was wrong about all of this?"

"All of what?" Tile asked.

Evan sighed deeply. "Benny."

"What do you mean?"

"What if Benny really is in the wrong here? What if I just want to defend him because he's my friend and he's really smart and I don't want to see him get hurt? What if they are just doing their job and Benny really is a threat to all the good work they have done?" It almost hurt to say these words, but Evan also felt a weight lifted off his shoulders, as though he had suspected it all along and finally saying it made him feel so much better.

"Do you think he is wrong?" the professor pressed.

"The things that he is doing don't line up with the MEBA system."

"So either the system is wrong or Benny is wrong and the system is fine."

"But if Benny is wrong, then he is a criminal and deserves to go to jail."

"Have you considered that both Benny and the MEBA system are both good? I am no philosophy teacher, but you may be looking at this a bit too straightforwardly."

"They can't both be right. If the system is correct and they are able to properly tell if people are doing the right thing or the wrong thing, then destroying the ability for it to tell right from wrong is obviously wrong. If Benny is correct, then the system as a whole needs to be destroyed and all of the data with it."

"What is the point of the MEBAs?"

"To show us when we do something wrong and report it to everyone so that others can know how good you are."

"Do you think that others really know how good you are?"

"Of course they do. Otherwise, what is the point of a MEBA score?"

"So a score is only good so that others can know how good you are?"

"Yeah, I guess so."

"Who controls the MEBA system?"

"Isn't it sort of self-regulated?"

"It is now. Who set the system up to begin with?" It was now that all of Professor Tile's questions began to sink in. For Benny, it wasn't a question about whether or not the system could properly report guilt, it was whether or not the system *should* report it.

Evan sat with a strangely free conscience for the first time in a while. Then, his mind snapped back into its more naturally regulated way of thinking. "But, don't I need to have some kind of consequence for my actions?"

"You are too smart to be persuaded by people like me, Evan." Tile sat back as best she could in the light blue chair. She wanted to tell him more, but held back for a bit. Evan was indeed a brilliant student and a good person; he would most certainly understand the moral puzzle soon enough. "I think you have learned all the microbiology you need from me today."

"You can't just leave me. What should I do?"

Tile looked at him with a deepness that can only come from a teacher who understands their student. She stepped towards the door to leave, looked back at Evan and spoke softly. "You focus a lot on what you should or should not do."

Evan rose up in anger. "That's the point!" He actually yelled at his professor, but was too worked up to stop. "What good am I if I am not doing the right thing?"

Professor Tile just looked at him and smiled. The door from behind her was opened by the guard who had seen her stand up.

She turned around and walked out, hoping that Evan would understand exactly what he needed.

Evan stewed on the edge of his bed, mad at Tile for not giving him the answer, mad at himself for choosing to come to this place, mad at Benny for not letting him finish his dream. He felt alone again, like he had when Benny had first disappeared. Similarly, his only comfort was to soak the side of his pillow with tears of frustration until he fell back asleep.

CHAPTER 6

Ties and Decisions

No dream. He wished there was another dream. Maybe if he had gotten enough answers, Evan thought, he could piece all of this together and it could make sense. But all he got was a good night's rest and it was still early afternoon. He ordered a sandwich from his clipboard, ate it quietly, and tried to distract himself with reading.

While he read, he began to watch everyone. Mr. Crib at his desk seemed as robotic as always. The guards seemed bored, except for the one at the end of the hall, who Evan felt was the only realistic person in this whole place. That guard was always looking around, scratching his leg, or fidgeting. It was almost fun to watch someone who couldn't get comfortable, Evan thought.

The elevator opened, revealing Mr. Pierce, who instantly made eye contact with Evan and began walking towards the room he was staying in. Evan stood up, as one would when being introduced to an important figure. Mr. Pierce tapped in the code to his room, twisted the nob, and walked in, sitting himself in the chair that Evan had gotten up from. He motioned for Evan to have a seat on his bed, which the student did somewhat slowly as though he was trying to size up his competition before a fight.

"Mr. Roman, thank you for coming here to the AMA. I understand… that your needs have been met and your… safety has been ensured. I would like to have a discussion about… your roommate Benny and his… potential to undermine the MEBA system."

Evan sat as calmly as he could while his insides churned. "Okay." He said shyly.

"Please understand, Mr. Roman, that our intentions are to see if what… Benny was doing could be interpreted or confirmed to be an act of rebellion against the MEBA system and the structure of justice that has been firmly set in place… by that system. The repercussions of Benny's… supposed actions would be immense and would affect many people in a negative way. We simply want to protect those who are properly following the Guidelines of Proper Living."

There were copies of this book Mr. Pierce referenced pretty much everywhere. It laid out what would and what would not trigger the MEBA system to show guilt. It was updated every week to keep up with potential new ideas or concepts of guilt. Evan had a copy by his bedside. He would look through it, especially when he felt like he had done something that may qualify as wrong. About once a week when he was in high school, he would wake up with it dimly lit in his hands. It was his lifestyle to watch his back and make sure his decisions didn't catch up to him.

Evan finally responded after thinking for a few seconds. "I understand."

Mr. Pierce continued. "Please tell me in as much detail… as you feel comfortable, what kind of projects Benny was working on, especially if you think they may have the potential... to be destructive to the MEBA system as it currently stands."

A pause filled the air as Evan thought of how to respond to the question. He knew he had to choose his words wisely so he wouldn't be lying but also wouldn't put his friend in trouble since he didn't really know Benny's intentions. "Benny is the smartest guy I know. He would often work with his personal MEBA, as well as mine without my permission, to learn about how it operated."

"What kind of work would he do on your MEBAs?"

"Mostly funny things, like overriding the numbers to display a winking face. Things like that."

"Did he ever change your score?"

"My score has been stuck on the same number for a long time. I don't know for certain whether or not it was because of something Benny did. It may have just been a malfunction."

"Did Benny ever give you access... to anything that could have been used to help the system malfunction?"

Evan took a deep breath. "I don't think so." He knew that was probably a lie, but he convinced himself that he didn't know what the blueprints were for since he hadn't actually constructed it yet.

"How long have you been friends with Benny?"

"Since the start of college, about three and a half years."

"How much did Benny discuss with you his goals in... tampering with the MEBAs?"

"We were roommates for over three years. We talked a lot. He never said anything about trying to destroy or wreck the system. We talked about things that were and weren't fair. We talked about justice and virtue. We talked about how we could one day change the world for the better with our knowledge. He never said he wanted to shut down MEBAs."

"How do you think he intended... to change the world?"

"I don't know," Evan responded defensively.

"Do you think he wanted to get a normal job and work and have a family?"

"Doesn't sound like him. He wasn't exactly someone who seemed like they were going to settle down and be normal."

"So I hear you saying that he wanted to find his own way of changing the world and that you often talked about fairness, justice, and virtue. Very... interesting." Evan thought that if Mr. Pierce didn't have a speech impediment, he would have sounded evil when he said "very interesting" the way he did.

"That's correct, but I don't think it means he would do something like rebel against the MEBA system or what it stood for. He often mentioned that he liked it a lot."

"Did he ever mention... wanting to change it?"

"He did say he wanted to make it better."

"I see." Mr. Pierce sat back in the chair, typing on the computer he brought with him. He typed for an uncomfortably long time, even to the point where Evan felt like he should maybe ask him if he planned on leaving. Before he could get out a polite way to ask if they were done, Mr. Pierce stood, offered his hand for a handshake, and began to leave the room. Before he left, he turned to face Evan once again. Adjusting his entire body to line up with

Evan's, the narrow man stated he "would be have a conversation with Mr. Crib... about a potential reward they could give to Evan for his assistance in clarifying... the matter."

As the door closed behind him, Evan sat in silence, replaying the conversation over and over again in his head. As he did so, his eyes began to dart around the room, looking for something to focus on. Eventually, they found Mr. Crib, rising slowly and purposefully from his desk at the end of the hallway. He gathered up a large stack of papers and started walking with them down the hallway. Evan hadn't seen those papers before and Mr. Crib's desk (from what he remembered) was always very clean and tidy, never having papers on it before. The stocky gentleman strode over to the door with the black furniture, put his passcode in, and opened the door himself. The room was too far away and through too many thick pieces of plexiglass for Evan to tell what was going on. It looked like they were sitting and talking and it was all Evan could do to imagine what they could be talking about.

About an hour passed with Evan still glued to Mr. Crib and the man in the black room. It seemed that they might talk all night. They were only interrupted by the nervous guard, who walked to the door of the room when he saw that Mr. Pierce had entered through the elevator. Evan hadn't even noticed Mr. Pierce and shot a glance over when the guard pointed it out.

With the tall, slow-talking gentleman were two girls, who seemed to be about the same age as Evan, if not a little bit older. They were both a bit taller than Evan, both wide-eyed, and both with small, slanted noses that made them look like know-it-alls. Looking like identical twins, the only striking difference between the two was their hair; one sported a longer, dirty blonde hair that was neatly straightened down to her upper back. The other had very dark brown hair and had it cut shorter, just hanging over her neck and flaring out a bit.

Mr. Crib left his conversation with the man in the black room and made his way slowly back to his desk, slowly down the hallway, and slowly into a conversation with the two girls. It seemed very similar to the conversation that Evan had with him when he first arrived a couple of days ago. Evan wondered why they were here and what they thought about the MEBAs and if they could be friends and what Benny would think about them.

Down the long hallway, Evan watched as Mr. Crib and the girls talked with each guard all the way down, just as he had done when he arrived. After the conversations, Crib motioned with his somewhat stumpy arm towards Evan's room and he led the girls where he pointed. Arriving at the red room next to Evan's, Crib typed in his passcode and gently opened the door, swinging it wide for the two girls.

"Oh gosh, I'm staring," he said to himself as he watched. "They are going to think I'm really creepy." He turned abruptly to avoid any eye contact and pretended to read the biggest book he had near him. Peering over the spine of the book, he watched as Mr. Crib showed them their room and helped Mr. Pierce to get their belongings to them. Matching suitcases were rolled in and given to them while Mr. Crib explained the clipboard. He shook the hands of the twins, wiped his own in a handkerchief and gently closed the door, making his way back to the black room to continue to discuss the stack of papers with the other man.

The twins seemed to be talking for a few minutes when they glanced over towards Evan, who at that point was clearly not interested in the weighty book in his lap. Embarrassed enough from knowing that he shouldn't be staring, he turned bright red when they called attention to him by pointing. The shorter haired twin gave him a friendly wave, but Evan forgot to wave back until it was too late to be considered normal.

"They must think I'm an idiot," he told himself as he sat there wishing his book was more interesting. Another handful of minutes passed. He wanted to talk to the girls, but he didn't know how to start a conversation. It was then that the long-haired twin walked over to the see-through glass and motioned for him to come over. Evan's legs stood him up and walked over; he tried not to seem too interested when he looked at them and said hi.

They waved back.

He could see them talking, but when he couldn't hear them, he realized that the rooms were soundproof. How was he supposed to get to know them? While he was trying to figure out a way, the short-haired twin grabbed one of the books on the shelf. Even thought that it looked like a philosophy book of some sort, thick with words and long-ended arguments. From her back pocket, she took a pen and began writing on the cover of the book. After a few moments, she held it up for Evan to read.

"Who are you? Why are you here? How long have you been here for?"

Evan went to grab a book to write in. He first reached for the big book he had been pretending to read, only to realize that he didn't want to hold that up continuously. He instead grabbed an old fantasy novel titled "Silvan's Travels" and opened to the blank pages in the back before the back cover. He scribbled, trying to see if the twins were watching or not between sentences.

"My name is Evan, I was brought here because my best friend found a way to destroy the MEBA system and they want to stop him from doing so…" He paused. Was this part of their plan? To get him to talk to a couple of girls? Is that why they seemed to be his age, so they could try to persuade him to talk? He continued to write, even though these ideas began to stir in his head. He turned to the front of the book and wrote down two questions to show the girls.

'Who are you? Why are you here?"

The two girls looked confused/worried and wrote back. "It's a long story, but the short of it is that the AMA thinks we know people who are trying to destroy the MEBA system."

Evan immediately flipped back to the back page he was writing on, finished his thoughts, and held it up for the girls to read.

"My name is Evan, I was brought here because my best friend found a way to destroy the MEBA system and they want to stop him from doing so. They seem to be taking good care of me because they think I can convince him to give them the secrets to undo-ing the work. I've only been here for a couple of days."

Evan smiled as they read it, thinking that someone else was in the same boat as he was and finally feeling a little bit normal. The girls held the book back up with arrows pointing left and right and names next to the arrows.

← Diane Celeste →

The shorter haired twin stood to the right of the book and the longer haired twin stood to the left. "That one must be Celeste," Evan thought. "And that one is Diane." He wrote in his book quickly.

→ Evan

He stood next to the book and both twins laughed. He realized that it was the first time he had heard laughing in weeks, although in this instance he saw the laugh instead of hearing it. He and Benny had always been laughing together, even when they disagreed. He spent the whole day trying to communicate with the twins, quickly realizing that he was writing too big and too sloppily and using up too much space in the margins of the books. Back and forth they exchanged information. They had mentioned their friend Arch and how he thought that the MEBA system had some sort of government conspiracy behind it. They said that they were questioned by the army but they honestly didn't know anything and when the army realized it, they flew them here to keep them safe from whatever organization was trying to debunk the validity of the MEBA system.

"Do you think the system is good?" Evan found himself asking the girls.

"Do you mean 'does it work' or should it exist'?"

"Both."

It was the first time the twins didn't start writing immediately. The entire time, Diane had been holding the book and writing in it while Celeste looked over her shoulder and talked. When Evan showed them his question, however, Celeste went to grab her own book and began writing like Diane had. They both seemed to regress in maturity as they began to compete with each other over finishing what they were writing. Diane finished first and slammed her book against the see-through wall.

"Of course it is good. Look at what it has done. People are safer knowing where the boundaries in their life are. Those that can't deal with consequences are the only ones who don't like the MEBA system. The rest of us shouldn't have to suffer because some people are immature and can't handle following the rules."

As soon as Evan finished reading Diane's message, Celeste pressed her book against the wall as well and gestured for him to read hers.

"Of course it shouldn't exist. It is a program that hurts people when they make mistakes. Everyone has made mistakes and hurting people beyond what mistakes already do is just awful. It is just a program that enables some people to control others, and that cannot be good."

Suddenly Evan felt trapped as both twins began to stare at him as if to say "which of us do you agree with?" He didn't really have an answer for the unspoken question. He did like that the MEBA system told him how to do well and be successful, but he also really enjoyed the freedom he had felt recently when Benny has stopped his MEBA from tracking his actions. He hadn't really seen it hurt anybody in particular, but he could see that happening. Not knowing what to do, Evan just shrugged at the twins. Maybe they would figure it out themselves.

A knock on the wall interrupted the awkward moment, startling Evan and the twins. The guard across the room from the twins was at their door. Evan just stared dumbfounded, like it was the only thing on tv and he was stuck on a couch. Diane wrote to him a moment later.

"We have a visitor coming to see us."

"Did you request one?" Evan wrote back in the small space he had left on the bottom of his book.

"No, they said it was someone who knew us." Diane responded in her book. She then wrote again, "do you think someone is going to pick us up from here?"

Evan had not yet considered that they might be able to get out if someone comes to get them. Who would come to get him out? Does his family even know he's here? What about Jeremy? Is he back with the family? Would he be allowed to go back knowing what he knows? What does he even know?

The elevator door opened and in walked Professor Tile. "What was she doing back here?" Evan continued to ask himself unanswerable questions in his head. She strode to the twins' door and was let in by the guard. Evan began scribbling as fast as he could, holding the book up to the clear wall.

"How do y'all know Professor Tile?"

He would have to wait for his response because the twins were embracing his teacher in an enveloping hug, one on each side of her. For a moment, he felt completely alone again, the new companionship of the two girls faded quickly in the light of what seemed to be a real relationship between them and his instructor. The only person he imagined he would hug that much was Benny or Jeremy. After a few moments, Diane wrote in her book and put it up to the wall.

"She's our mum."

Evan jaw dropped, and he tried to make any sense of that. He almost didn't believe it, but soon he started noticing the family traits that they shared, the wide-set eyes and the narrow shoulders especially. He imagined that the twins had the same accent his professor had this whole time. He began to study the three of them, trying to read their lips but getting drowned by just watching them interact with each other. It was endearing to see; even though he knew he was staring awkwardly, Evan couldn't stop. An epiphany came over him as he observed the family gathering for the first time in what was probably months. What was happening in front of him was good… genuinely good. It wasn't morally good; it was just good. Diane and Celeste, who were ready to argue over who was right about MEBAs, put down their opinion for a while and recognized what was really important. They did not purposely stop disagreeing, and Evan knew that without a second thought, but it did mean that something was more important than their agreement. Their MEBA scores would not likely recognize this and a report would never be made. However, it was clear to Evan that this was something special.

Lost in the desire to see his own family, his thoughts drifted away from the twins and back into his own head, which seemed more and more empty. Evan wanted to see Jeremy; not to find out what he learned, but just to see him. He missed Jeremy for the first time. He missed his inquisitive nature and his childlike desire to be loved by Evan. He missed being looked up to and looking after Jeremy. He missed the meals around the family table and the small jabs at each other between bites of chicken. Suddenly, embarrassment came over him as though he should not have been watching Professor Tile's family talking. He went about his own business, writing down a list of things he wanted from the guards: 2 peanut butter and honey sandwiches, another meeting with Professor Tile, and a phone call with Jeremy. He also put on there one final thing, knowing well and good that it was unlikely to happen: he would like to leave. There wasn't a reason he could think of that would keep Mr. Crib or Mr. Pierce from letting him go. He had already spoken and told them as much as he felt like he was going to. Still, he felt like he was unable to leave, so writing it down didn't really excite him as much as he would have hoped it would.

When he looked up again, Professor Tile was already leaving the Twin's room, giving a polite wave to Evan as she walked off, the latter waving back somewhat automatically. He picked up the closest book he hadn't scribbled through and asked Celeste and Diane through his writing to explain their relationship with his professor and why she came to visit. Celeste took her turn writing out the story while Diane sat next to her on the bed. It seemed like they were going to give Evan the full story about his favorite professor, but that would require patience on his part.

While Evan watched the two pen their thoughts, the guard across from his room came and took the list he had made, walked off with it, handed it to Mr. Crib, and re-took his position when he was finished. A few moments later, which passed quickly because Evan had a monologue with himself about the likelihood of him leaving, the sandwiches were delivered and a note with them. The envelope was so crisp it seemed to have come straight from the factory, sealed perfectly and creased such that it gave Evan a paper cut when he grabbed it. Looking up at the guard, he asked quickly for a bandaid to cover his now bleeding index finger.

"You will have to fill out a form." The guard simply replied.

"Really?" Evan questioned how reasonable that was. After not getting a reply, he finally reached down and picked up a form and put "1 bandaid" on the form, handed it to the guard, and sat down to hold his finger for the next 3 minutes while he waited for the bandaid to be delivered.

While waiting for the bandaid, Evan opened up the envelope, doing his best not to get blood on the edges. The note inside was typed and simple:

"At this time, we are unable to comply with your request to speak with your brother Jeremy. At this time, Professor Tile has expressed a lack of desire to come and meet with you. Thank you for understanding. Mr. Crib."

This was the first time it struck Evan that he might not be in a place where he is actually safe, but rather captive. "How?" he thought to himself and he robotically accepted the band-aid the guard brought over. He thought about how nothing that Mr. Crib or Mr. Pierce said was alarming, concerning, or hard to think about. All they asked for from Evan was his participation in trying to stop something bad from happening. Evan wanted to help. He wanted to be a good person. He wanted to be good enough to raise his MEBA score, have a normal job, and live a normal life. He wanted not to be tied to things that were frustrating, hard, or confusing. Sitting back and glancing around the room, he realized that he finally got what he wanted. This place was simple, obvious, and never had surprises for him. It was safe. "This place sucks," Evan said out loud for the first time. It felt good, so he said it again and again. He began jumping and stomping around the room, throwing stuff on the floor, shouting at the top of his lungs "sucks sucks sucks!"

At the end of his tantrum, exhausted and out of breath from jumping, dancing and haphazardly creating a tornado of papers, Evan just smiled and looked up; he noticed the twins once again, but this time they were staring at him. They both giggled, then laughed out loud. He laughed with them, feeling absolutely euphoric for no reason at all. He shouldn't be happy; he was nonetheless. On the floor lay parts of books, cords from his computer, and sprinkles of blood that has escaped from his bandage in the commotion.

The guard across from his room was approached by Mr. Crib, then walked methodically over to Evan's door. "Excuse me," he politely spoke. "Mr. Crib would like to speak to you in the other room please."

Even knew he was in trouble. How could he not be? No matter; he was in the sort of mood where what other people thought didn't really matter. Logic had completely been abandoned for what seemed to him like a much needed breath of fresh air. The guard walked him down the hall to Mr. Crib's desk. Mr. Crib stood up, buttoned his well-pressed suit, and calmly said "Follow me, Mr. Roman."

The words fell flat before "Mr. Roman", having little to no effect on his mood. Once they may have struck distaste, fear, or even humor in Evan's mind; now nothing. The words seemed to just hang in the air as Evan watched Mr. Crib gather himself, re-button his suit jacket, and stride cautiously to the side of the room. It was the same side that the guards were lined up on, opposite of the rooms where the people stayed. The square-jawed man approached the only door that wasn't currently protected by one of the guards and opened it. Evan remembered this room from his dream. This is the room that the group left through before he woke up. Walking in, the same staircase from his dream was standing there, tall and welcoming, spiraling up and down the white-washed corridor. On the right, another door waited patiently; Mr. Crib guided Evan to proceed through it. The young boy did so, despite wanting to climb the spiralled steps on the other side of the small hallway.

The room inside was blank, save for a couple of bookshelves, a large computer that seemed to take over the wall opposite the entrance, a small bed, and a table with three chairs set on three of its sides.

"Make yourself comfortable," Mr. Crib gave instruction, following up with a question for his guest. "Would you like to rest for a while after your tirade?

"No, I'm good," the college student replied somewhat aggressively. He didn't mean for it to sound weird, but saying so might make things even more awkward than they seemed to be becoming.

"Very well, then," Mr. Crib continued. "I'm sure a young man of your intelligence understands what is about to happen."

"Am I going to be punished?"

"No. Not at all. Whatever gave you that suggestion?"

"I did sort of trash the room you gave me."

"It was your room. Why would I be upset if you wanted to keep your room more cluttered than I would keep it?"

"Well, it's not really my room though."

"Of course it is. Until you no longer need it, that room belongs to you and you alone." A brief pause hung over the room as Mr. Crib waited for Evan to say something. Since he chose not to, Mr. Crib continued. "By the end of our conversation, it will likely be time for dinner. Would you like for us to make something for you so that it is ready and you don't have to wait?"

Evan, still exhilarated from his outburst a few minutes ago, had an idea in his head; the thought spilled out of his head before he could tell himself it was too stupid to say. "I would like to have a steak, perfectly cooked medium well, topped with rainbow sprinkles. On the side, I want some string cheese, pre-pulled and in the shape of an infinity symbol. To drink, I want some purple orange juice and for dessert, a three pound chocolate Easter bunny." Mr. Crib just stared at him for a moment.

"Very well," the gentleman replied. "I shall put the request in immediately." He left the room for the briefest moment, just enough time to relay the information. While he did, the large computer, which was now behind Evan, began whirling, fans moving to cool the engines, a few lights blinking green and one blinking orange. Evan had a hard time not laughing at his own order.

Mr. Crib returned to the room and another gentleman came with him, one that Evan had not seen yet. This man was tall, but not as tall as Mr. Pierce, and board shouldered, but not as wide as Mr. Crib. He seemed quite a bit older than the similarly dressed co-workers that Evan had spoken to this whole time; his clustered chunks of brown hair, the only thing seemingly unpleasant about him, were wedged as best as he could get them underneath a dull-yellow derby hat. He wore the blankest stare upon his face, so much so that Evan thought he was doing it on purpose. In his hands were a stack of papers an inch and a half thick; the hands that held them had bandages all over, similar to Evan's in shape and size. Evan tried to count the number of times this new gentleman had been cut, but his thoughts were interrupted by Mr. Crib.

"This is Mr. Tab. He has prepared some paperwork for us to look through when we get the chance."

"Thank you, I guess." Evan wasn't really sure what to say. Likewise, the derby-hatted old man just stared, saying nothing back, completely blank. "The papers are sharp huh?" Evan tried to strike up a conversation, embarrassing himself by hearing his dad's words coming out of his mouth. Still no response.

"He keeps to himself, but we value his contribution to the Agency's work and particularly to our facility here." Mr. Crib complimented the older gentleman, who did not respond, but left from the room as though taking a cue from the director of a play.

Evan felt more relaxed than he had in a while until Mr. Crib placed his hand on the stack of papers and gently moved them towards the college student. Suddenly, he felt that he was in an interview of sorts and he had to make a good impression. His spine stiffened and his forehead began to moisten. Not sure what to do with his hands, he started fiddling with his left finger, pulling and pushing it to let out the anxiety that has so quickly come upon him. His foot began to tap nervously on the floor and he fixed his eyes as evenly as he could on the gentleman across from him.

Seeing the mental peril that the boy was going through, Mr. Crib spoke first to ease the unintended tension. "Do you know what we are doing in here Mr. Roman?"

"No," the reply trickled off Evan's lips.

"As you know, your friend Benny has put you into quite the predicament. This is simply an offer to get out of the nasty place he has put you." Evan sat in silence, knowing that he had to be careful when it came to talking about Benny. Mr. Crib continued. "I would like to offer you a job. You are clearly very intelligent and you have a strong background in technology from your collegiate course load. I think it is high time that you were rewarded for your hard work and dedication to knowledge. We here at the Agency of MEBA Affairs continue to work hard to maintain the balance of the world's MEBAs and ensure that when difficulties arise, they are handled with ease. We accept only the top MEBA scores in our company to continue the tradition of excellence with every passing day. When we run smoothly, the world runs smoothly. We can start you off your first year at $200,000 and full benefits."

Evan almost choked on his own spitle. "Are you serious?" he blurted out, only to collect himself and straighten his spine once more.

"Do I seem like someone who jokes around with his work?"

"I'm sorry sir," Evan realized when he caught his breath. "I cannot work for the AMA. My score is stuck at 37, and even before that, it wasn't nearly high enough to get a job here."

Mr. Crib raised his eyebrow the slightest bit, but it was more emotion than Evan had ever seen him show. "Mr. Roman, I don't quite think you understand. We are willing to change your MEBA score to where we think it truly belongs, and from the records we show, we have no reason to believe that your score should be anything but 100." Mr. Crib slid the documents over to Evan.

Opening the large stack of papers, Evan realized that most of the stack was data about himself. Each page was full of the decisions he has made through his life: times when he told the truth to his family, times when he performed well on school exams, and even times when he failed at something but tried his best. Page after page was nothing but glowing remarks about Evan's life, his choices, and the good things that had come from them. He was excited to see everything that he had worked for finally seem to pay off. The more he looked through the stack of his life, the more he realized something unusual. He had done some boneheaded things too, like yelling at his family in anger, promising to help someone out while fully knowing he was going to back out with a lame excuse, and even going behind his parents' back and leaving the house late at night to go see a movie with his friends. That last one, Evan thought to himself as he leafed through more papers of his good deeds, he felt awful about but he never got caught. His MEBA score went down by one the next day and he knew that it would come back to haunt him. No matter how hard he looked, he couldn't find any record of any of these choices. Where were his mistakes? His heart sank, dropping into the pit of his stomach. Evan looked up at Mr. Crib, who sat there staring. He knew that what was in front of him wasn't an accurate account of his life. It was only the good things. It was nice to have them lined up and reflect on how great some of his choices were, but it just wasn't the truth.

"I don't know what to say," Evan tried to process where the conversation was going, unable to predict Mr. Crib's ideas.

"Would you like some time to think about it? I can let you take a copy of these documents back to your room if you'd like. On the final pages, there is the job offer in question. It details all of the benefits of working for the AMA, both for you and for your family, and we even included Jeremy in that list, despite the fact that he is not actually a part of your family."

This made Evan outrageously mad for some reason, beyond the confusion and the difficulty understanding the situation he was in, having Jeremy called "not actually a part of [his] family" felt like the words of an angry man rather than someone who was as calm and collected as Mr. Crib seemed to be all the time. A sudden thought came over him before he lost his emotions. Perhaps Mr. Crib was trying to antagonize him, get under his skin, or maybe he was just testing him to see if he was really right for the AMA. Either way, Even focused all of his nervousness into his leg, hoping that Mr. Crib didn't notice.

"That seems like a good idea." Evan reached for the stack of papers.

"Oh please. Let me make you your own copy. It will only take 17 minutes." A pause hung in the air very briefly, after which, Mr. Crib walked gently to the door, opened it and said dutifully "Mr. Tab, would you please make a copy of Mr. Roman's personal documents? Thank you."

Without closing the door, he turned to Evan and gestured towards the door. "This way please. I will instruct Mr. Tab to bring the contract to your room." As Evan stood up, putting his nervousness into walking rather than shaking his leg, Mr. Crib stood in front of the door, looking down into Evan's stunned eyes. "Mr. Roman, it is with great excitement that I recommend taking this offer. You will finally be in the place you have wanted to be for years and you can leave your old life behind. No more questioning yourself. No more checking your MEBA every two hours. No more... nervousness."

Now Evan was certain that Mr. Crib was trying to get to him. He stared back, now furious, but trying to appear as peaceful as he could. "I said I will consider it," Evan declared in his most serious voice and shook Mr. Crib's hand as best as he could. He half-stormed, half-strolled out the door and down to this room. The guard that usually walks with him had a hard time keeping up walking through the long stretch of the hallway.

Evan moved quickly past the black room where the young man seemed to be reading through a large, brown book at his desk. The dark, curly hair of that man seems to recently have been cut and styled into a proper hairstyle, much different from the wild, shaggy mop that he had previously grown. Next was the dusty purple room, still vacant and seemingly inviting. In the middle of the long hallway was the green room, which now had someone inside of it, a young woman with dirty blonde hair down to the middle of her back. Evan could only guess that the dress she was in was for some sort of formal occasion, a lengthy black dress with one strap led down to uncomfortable looking high heels. As Evan passed this new member of the hall, he caught her eyes, which were angrily glaring at him. He quickened his pace, past the red room, and finally into the dusty blue room. To his surprise, the room was perfectly clean, his previous rampage was now completely undone. The bed sheets looked newly washed, the papers neatly stacked, and the blood from his cut was already bleached and the room returned to the way it was when he first arrived. He shot a glance at the twins, who were already writing in one of their books.

"They had 5 people in here cleaning up the place. It was impressive."

Evan grabbed one of his books and started scribbling, wondering. "Did you watch them?"

"Yes."

"Did they take anything?"

"Don't think so. Just the trash."

Evan's attention was caught again by the young woman in the green room. "Who is the new woman? Did she just come in?"

"Yes. No idea who she is, but we plan on finding out." Diane had a smirk in her eye when she showed this message to Evan.

"Did the men who cleaned my room stop to read my books or our conversations?"

"They just cleaned and left." The girls sat there in thought for a few moments before Celeste grabbed the book from Diane and wrote. "What did Mr. Crib want?"

The boy paused for a minute, thinking if there was a reason for him not to tell them about the conversation he had. Then he wrote and held up his book. "He offered me a job. A really good one."

Diane snatched the book back and wrote hurriedly, "no way! Seems a bit unfair." Celeste rolled her eyes after reading over her shoulder. "What did you say?" the book asked the next question.

"I said to let me think about it. Not sure what to do. They really haven't done anything wrong and I really like the MEBA technology. To work with it and help people live the right life is a good way to be safe and have a normal life. He basically offered me my dream job."

Celeste wrote back: "it sounds like a trap."

"What would the trap be?" Evan really was curious. He had no reason to believe that Mr. Crib had anything negative towards him. All he wanted was to find the truth about Benny's device and hopefully handle that situation quickly. Still, Celeste's question felt very real and very important to answer.

No one responded while the question hung in the air like rotten fruit, rolling in waves through the rooms until everyone was used to the scent. A knock at Evan's door snapped him out of a downward spiral of unending questions, none of which had definitive answers. It was his food. Evan laughed out loud as the guard brought in a plate with a nice juicy steak topped as cleanly as possible with rainbow sprinkles, string cheese that looked like an infinity symbol, and orange juice that looked like it had food coloring in it to make it purple. Finally, staring at him with beady eyes, a three pound chocolate bunny, taking up more than half the plate it was laying on. He wasn't sure if he should be amazed or confused by how quickly they got every single thing he wanted. The boy looked up to see the twins laughing tears as they watched him stare at his requested plate. He now realized that they needed context for how silly this looked, but knew that trying to explain it would only make him look even more ridiculous than he already seemed. Instead, with as much confidence and he could manage, he scribbled down "you should ask for candy corn" and held it up to the girls, who laughed out the last bit of air they had in their lungs. It was the first time since high school that Evan felt like he had true friends other than Benny.

Half a bunny's ear and most of a steak later, Evan was brought the copied stack of papers that contained his potential contract. With the heavy meal stuck in his stomach, he quickly nodded off while trying to read through the first few pages of the stack of papers.

CHAPTER 7

"37"

The buzzing and beeping sounds that Evan was so used to back at college woke him up and a quick glance around the room told him it was likely the middle of the night. Lights were dimmed, the twins were asleep in their room, and the guards were sitting down in their chairs. It seemed familiar to his dream, as though the dream had taken place on this night. Most of the details didn't make sense for that though. The buzzing was his MEBA, which was delicately placed on the table next to his computer. Evan walked over to it to look and staring back at him was a display of completely green lights. 100. The perfect score. He turned it around, looking to make sure it wasn't a glitch of some sort, placed it on his wrist, and examined it.

A scream, long, loud, and piercing, rang through the hallways of the building. "This feels more like the dream," Evan said to himself, looking for reactions from the guards. "Did they hear it? Are they ignoring it?" The personal conversation continued for a brief moment when another scream went up; it felt like it was filling up Evan's room. The girls next door, however, didn't seem to wake. Maybe this was all in his head. Suddenly, the scream stopped. He looked around, noticing nothing particularly different. What was he supposed to do? Going back to sleep was unlikely with the scream occupying his thoughts and he couldn't just leave. Evan decided to pick up his book and start writing down some thoughts.

Another scream. It was difficult to discern where the scream came from, even though it obviously didn't originate in the blue room. Confused and lost for ideas, he remembered that Benny would always count to himself when he was trying to think. "It's worth a shot." Evan told himself and he tried to calm down. 1, 2, 3,... He made it to fourteen before another scream rang through the room. Thrown off and still unsure of what to do, he started counting again. 24, 25, 26... 30, 31, 32... Another scream. He counted the seconds between screams... 1, 2, 3, ...25, 26, 27... Why was he even doing this? What good would come out of it? 34, 35, 36, 37...... another scream. It couldn't be. He started counting immediately again, trying to correct the first couple of seconds to get the timing right. 37 seconds again. In between the screams, Evan finally realized what he could write down to focus his mind. This was just like trying to break the firewalls around the corrupted file from the blueprints; the rush of emotions kept Evan's mind on organizing his thoughts.

37 - showed up first on my MEBA when Benny hacked into it. Stayed that way no matter what. Next, it was the last answer to the questions on Professor Tile's tests. They were always that way though, meaning that Tile's 37 came before Benny's. Was Benny stealing her number as a joke? It's something he would do, but it never felt that way. It was also the number used in Benny's files for the device. He had been working on that for how long? Was it before or after Tile's class? Now the screams; why are they exactly 37 seconds apart? Was Benny the one screaming? If so, what would he be trying to communicate with me? Does the number 37 mean

anything else? It was prime, but that didn't seem to connect to anything. 3 and 7 individually didn't have any special meaning to Benny or Tile, although they were prime as well.

By the time the screams stopped, Evan's notebook looked like he was trying to piece together an unsolved mystery. How long had it been? Evan looked at his computer for the time. About 20 minutes or so had passed. He didn't have anything else to write at the time. Evan did his best to fall asleep, his heavy eyes joining him after about an hour of stirring and thinking.

* * *

Evan woke up, his head pounding in pain. The blue room he was in, cleaned and perfected other than the tiny bit of slobber on his pillow, seemed to welcome him into a new day. The stack of papers that held his contract stared back at him as if to say that it was a great morning to make an important choice. Evan's heart groaned. He wasn't ready for that. He looked over to the room next to him, where the twins were eating breakfast, some sort of potato hash, bread with brown butter, and grapefruit juice in both glasses. When Diane noticed he was awake, she smiled and walked over, writing in her book.

"Marmite! They have Marmite!"

Evan looked confused.

Diane continued to scribble. "It's a yummy spread for your bread." Evan still looked confused. Then he remembered that just yesterday, he ordered a chocolate bunny for dessert. He smiled at Diane, giving her a thumbs up. She seemed satisfied with this and went to enjoy her breakfast.

Evan wasn't too hungry, so he just put some healthy cereal that his mom was always trying to get him to eat. When it came, he also frustratingly had to add milk and wait a minute or two before the guard brought that as well. As he lazily ate his food, Evan started flipping through the documents that had been delivered to him yesterday. Next to him, his MEBA flashed 100, as though to remind him of the gift that Mr. Crib and the AMA were giving to him.

A gentle knock at the door woke him from his reading stupor. He looked up to see Benny, standing there with a goofy grin on his face. Around his grin, bruises and cuts sunk into his cheeks, trying to keep him from smiling too much. The purple and black hues spread from his left cheek down to his neck and left shoulder. His ripped jeans and worn hoodie did their best to hide what had transpired, but the gaps in the clothes told the story of what happened last night.

"Benny!" Evan ran to the thick plastic door that kept him from his friend. "What happened?"

His friend only smiled bigger. "It's good to see you. How are you doing?" Through the thick wall, the words were muffled a little, so Benny's voice sounded a bit deeper and quieter, but Evan could still hear every word.

"ARE YOU JOKING?!" Evan shouted, calling the twins attention to the conversation. "Who cares about me right now!?" realizing he was gathering more attention than Benny probably wanted, he quieted down and began to talk just below the volume of a normal conversation. "Did they beat you up?"

"Yeah, pretty hard. They felt that I was hiding something from them; they saw that as lying and my MEBA score dropped so far, my counter couldn't keep up." Benny laughed a bit at that, somewhat infuriating Evan. "It fell so low that, according to the law, they were able to beat me up with no consequence of their own. I now have a score of 3. Kind of beats your 37 huh?" Benny laughed again, harder this time until it clearly hurt his face.

"This isn't funny, Benny!" Evan started to raise his voice again before catching himself. He now felt even more awkward that he was offered a perfect MEBA score to work for the people who were doing this to Benny. How could he have been so stupid? Didn't he realize that only horrible people could do such a thing to another person? He had been bribed, and now that he realized it, everything became clearer. He determined in his mind that he would never take that job now, no matter what they tried to give him.

Benny looked Evan straight in the eyes, as though to read his thoughts. He then smiled and asked "What does a score of 100 mean to you Evan?"

Evan blurted out "It means I'm finally good enough at something to be successful in this stupid world!" Slowly, Evan backed away from the door, taking a step to rethink what escaped his mouth. The pause that filled the air was palpable. Benny just kept staring and smiling, as though nothing Evan said or would ever say would change the way he thought about his friend. When Evan finally locked eyes with Benny again, he saw it. That dumb look of being accepted, of being enough, staring right back at him on the other side of the door. Evan was undone; tears leapt down his face and clung to the top of his wrinkled t-shirt. "Why are you even friends with me?" he finally sniffled out after a minute.

"I like who you are," his friend responded. "I like how intense you are about pretty much everything. I like how you love Jeremy so much and how you talk with your family. I like that you work hard even when you don't understand everything. I like that you are great at one-on-one conversations, even when they aren't with me. I like that you are way too emotional for a college guy."

Evan laughed at that one. Everything Benny said felt so true and honest. It felt real. Unlike the large stack of papers that stated every single action that Evan did, Benny's words actually did something in Evan. It made him realize the lack of importance of whether or not he could judge himself to be enough. Wiping away the leftover tears and snot from crying and laughing, Evan looked up at his friend and asked, "What now?"

"Oh yeah, that reminds me." Benny chuckled in a way that made Evan feel uncomfortable.

"What now Benny?" Evan asked again.

The bruise under Benny's left eye raised a bit with his cheeks. He spoke firmly and calmly. "This conversation was a request of mine. Mr. Crib, Mr. Tab, and I were talking and after we came to an agreement, they asked me if there was anything I wanted before they carried out their side of the deal."

Evan paused for a moment. "Benny, what was the deal?"

"I'm going to be put on trial."

"You're WHAT?!" Evan shouted, forgetting his previous ideas of staying quiet.

"Well, I did sort of mess with the MEBA system, didn't I?"

"Yeah, I guess, but it was only in fun right? Surely you can apologize and return..." Evan's thoughts and voice trailed off together. He realized what was going on. The clarity of mind he had found when he chose to "side" with Benny rather than the AMA kicked in. Like a puzzle, the pieces finally started lining up. All of those nights of he and Benny talking about making an impact on the world, doing good, being good. Evan always felt that it was the classic college student's conversation. He never really thought that either of them would become something that would actually change the world. Benny did. The train of thoughts linked themselves to each other, providing connections where there used to be only questions. When Evan looked back at Benny, he matched the heartfelt intensity of his eyes; Evan finally understood.

"You had this planned all along, didn't you?"

Benny smiled reassuringly. It was the only communication Evan needed.

"You want to be here... you want to go to trial? Why? What's the point? Oh no.."

Benny smiled again, although this one didn't make Evan feel quite as good.

"You know there is no way you are winning this trial, so what's going to happen when you lose?

Benny stopped smiling, instead looking his friend directly in his eyes. "I need to do this. Just know that I'm okay with this. No matter what." With that, Benny lifted up his hand, which was swollen and had marks on it, like they had been tied with a rough cord. The guard across the hall walked over.

Evan, seeing the moving guard, tried to finish whatever conversation needed to be finished. "Wait, Benny. What do you want me to do? I had a weird dream about you. When can I see you next? What does 37 mean?" Each question seemed to hit the glass between them, stopping before they made it to Benny's ears. Benny quietly backed up, turned, and walked towards the room near Mr. Crib's desk, the same one that Evan had received his contract in. Mr. Crib, who had been sitting silently at his desk staring into the middle of the hallway, stood and followed Benny and the guard.

Lost in thought for a few moments, Evan snapped back to himself when he realized that the twins were probably watching the whole thing. But when he turned around, they weren't even paying attention; rather their bodies were turned to the young woman in the green room, looking like they were communicating with her in some way. That was fine, Evan thought to himself as he turned to his bed

A couple of minutes later, the twins turned back to Evan, who was writing down as much of his conversation with Benny as he wanted to share. He didn't really want to put much down, but felt it was important for them to know that Benny was going on trial but that he didn't care and wanted to lose. When he finally looked up, having wiped away any leftover tears and putting on a face that looked as put together as it could, the twins were staring at him as though they could see right through him. He turned red, trying not to think of himself as embarrassed by his emotional state. Eventually he took the book up to them and showed them what was happening to Benny. As they read it, Diane started to shed some tears as well, giving great comfort to Evan and they stood with this dark news among them. Celeste, on the other hand, grew angry, saying "they can't do this" over and over again under her breath. She stormed over and wrote on the request paper quickly.

"I asked to see Mum again," she whispered to her sister.

"Do you think there is something she can do about Benny?" Diane responded.

"It's worth a shot. What other ideas do you have?"

Diane has no response. As she turned to look up, she saw Evan turning to his computer as something had popped up on the screen.

Evan dedicated his whole attention to what he began to see happening; a live-feed was beginning. It was a room with Benny sitting in a chair in the middle, large screens on one side of the room. The camera was angled in such a way that it hid the door and about a quarter of the room with it. The picture, however, was crystal clear, sharp and more colorful than he could imagine. For some reason, he felt like he was seeing Benny for the first time. Since he knew that his friend had planned this all along, he felt like he was part of the secret, part of the answer. He didn't really understand what the question was, but he knew that whatever was really happening was good. Really good. Truly good.

Benny was standing in the middle of the room while two men, one that looked to be Mr. Tab and the other looked like of the guards from the hallway, were hooking up wires from the large computer to Benny's fingers and his chest. Evan recognized that the places that they were connecting them in were key parts of the MEBA system, often measuring guilt through movement in the hands, heartbeat, and pulse levels. As this was happening, Benny looked directly at the camera and smiled, as if to say hi to his friend who he knew was watching.

Behind Benny, the wall lit up with a screen that displayed nine faces, different people with different eyes, different noses, different teeth, different chins, and different skin tones. Each of them as they appeared lifted their hands to show them on the screens. Evan had never seen something like that before and did not know the point of the gesture. The two men started to push wires into Benny's skin, similar to a nurse beginning to draw blood or give medicine. One of the wires, a thin, grey wire, seemed to be shoved pretty deeply into the chest area. Evan knew that it was going to connect to the central MEBA input near the heart. It was one that could also trigger a switch that could reduce his heart rate to lethal levels. As he watched, sweat began to trickle down his forehead.

A voice came from the area the camera wouldn't show; it was gravelly and quick, making it hard to understand unless you were fully paying attention. "We will now begin Benny's trial. Will those in attendance, please state your name and MEBA score for audio and video confirmation?"

One by one the different faces gave their names, followed by perfect MEBA scores.

"Justin Klack; 100."

"Adel Firit; 100."

"Hadiya Einsberger; 100."

"Nima Jones; 100."

"Rashida Kellin; 100."

"Nemesio Rodriguez; 100."

"Saladin Amin; 100."

"Yi Tran; 100."

"Ashtad Calyndos, 100"

It wasn't until halfway through the list that Evan realized that he would have a 100 score if he had accepted the job. Would he have been asked to be a juror? Did these people earn their scores or were they given to them by the company? Were these all just people who worked for the AMA? The sweat turned to large drops as he thought through how much control the AMA may have had in making this trial happen, even to the point of guaranteeing an outcome.

"That's okay," Evan forced himself to say. "This was part of Benny's plan."

The voice once again droned from the unseen corner of the room. "Thank you. Benny, before the trial begins, you now have an opportunity to speak on your behalf. You are being accused of developing technology and intent to implement said technology to shut down the MEBA system. Would you care to comment?"

Evan watched as his friend stayed silent. The twins behind him knocked on the wall to get his attention, but he was far too focused to give them even the slightest acknowledgement.

The voice spoke one more time. "This is your final opportunity to speak Benny. Do you have any comments on the accusation brought against you?" Silence. "Let the recording show that Benny refuses to comment or defend his accusations." Evan watched as all nine of the jurors seemed to be taking notes, writing down in the pauses the voice gave them.

"According to the testimony of Benny's friend and roommate, Evan Roman, Benny, and I am quoting here, 'work[ed] with his personal MEBA, as well as mine without my permission' and that Benny 'talked about how we could one day change the world.' When asked about what sort of things they wanted to change, Mr. Roman stated very clearly that the topics they would speak about were always those of justice, fairness, and virtue. I submit to you that Benny claimed he wanted to change the world and specifically change the justice in the world. Now since the AMA and the use of MEBAs is the current justice in the world and there is both spoken and physical evidence that Benny had the opportunity and the capability to operate on MEBAs in a way so as to change their output, it is clear that at the very least Benny had all of the potential to try to destroy and overwrite the system that is currently keeping the world properly accountable for their actions." A pause hung in the air while the jury took notes, each of them raising the back of their hand to the camera to show that they were finished. The voice continued. "Benny, do you have any comments on these words? Very well. Please note that the defendant chose not to speak against the testimony."

This process continued on for some time, calling on the words of people Evan hadn't heard of. Each person would say similar things when it came to his abilities, but completely different things if they spoke of his personality. It was as though they met a different person with the same skill set.

One spoke of a young man from high school who helped them fix their broken car, resetting the electrical scale that was thrown off during a lightning storm. They mentioned that the young man said his name was Ben and that he wanted to help as many people as possible and that he thought he had a way of helping everyone in the world.

Another voice, this one older and female, spoke into the room, saying that they lived next to Benjamin (as they had always called him) for a few years. They mentioned that he was always bringing them cookies and sitting in the living room with their kids, and that he asked the most interesting questions. When pressed about the questions he would ask, they were along the lines of "how can technology tell us if we are good or not?" Very high level thinking from such a young child, she mentioned in her testimony.

One person just called him "Nenjaman" because that was his name on the game they played together. They said that Benny had often found loopholes around the game design that let the players on his team get end game rewards at the start of the game. A lot of people that played the game hated this and the game had to be shut down because everyone was doing the same shortcuts.

It took Evan a while to realize how many people Benny probably knew before coming to college. He wasn't offended as much as taken aback. It was peaceful to know that the Benny that Evan got to know really was a great guy, which is what each testimony seemed to say about him. Maybe, just maybe, Benny wanted to go to trial so that they could see that he was good and a benefit to the AMA. Maybe Benny was just doing things his own way and he could now work together with Evan.

"We have reached a verdict." The screen shifted focus to the nine jurors, of which Nima was speaking.

"Proceed," the voice replied.

"We find the defendant guilty of the charge of conspiring to destroy and uproot the MEBA system and the AMA and sentence him to death."

The blood from Evan's face drained, his eyes nearly rolled back, and he lost a moment or two of time. "It couldn't actually be," he thought to himself when he got his mind right. He turned to the twins, who were crying as well, seeing Evan's reaction and the screen's words showing that Benny was given a guilty verdict.

The voice from overhead stated plainly, "The verdict of guilty has been reached by the jury brought in to judge the actions and intentions of Benny. The sentence will be carried out tomorrow at 3:00pm. All personnel please prepare the room to carry out the sentence against Benny. Thank you."

The next few moments were a blur for Evan; he watched as two guards came in and led Benny away from the chamber, the voice the corner thanked each individual who was on the jury, letting them know that they would follow up with them. The voice then asked their permission to include them in the official writing of the trial for documentary purposes. Each of them gave permission without hesitation. The voice thanked each individual once more before inviting them to take their leave. All of this took about thirty minutes to go through so meticulously, but it felt like one or two minutes to Evan as he sat and tried his best to breathe deeply without crying.

Gathering himself together, Evan ran through the options he felt like he had. He dismissed the idea of trying to overturn the verdict, since he had convinced himself that Benny actually wanted that outcome. Then he dismissed the thought of just trying to leave or escape (escape didn't feel like the right word; he wasn't a captive right?). That wouldn't really do any good. He thought about doing nothing as well, which actually seemed like a pretty good option considering he didn't feel as though anything was in his control anyway. Finally, he settled on the only thing he knew to be a step he felt safe with, even if it didn't do much for Benny right now. On the clipboard, he wrote down that he would like to see Mr. Crib about the potential contract he was presented with yesterday.

As Evan looked next door, Celeste and Diane were talking to each other, the former consoling the latter as they did so. Evan guessed that Celeste was the emotionally stronger of the two and Diane was a bit more like he was when it came to expressing himself. Celeste held up a book with words written in it: "They aren't letting Mum come to see us."

"Why not?" Evan mouthed his words and shrugged.

"???" was scribbled quickly in the margins.

Benny's friend felt badly for them, but he convinced himself that at least they had each other and that meant they were better off than he was. He wrote in the book, "I have nothing now; no Benny, no job, and a family that will probably be scared of me because of everything that has happened. I don't want to hurt their scores and I'm sure I will if I hang around them too much."

As he wrote, he thought to himself that maybe the best thing for him to do is just to do his best, obey the laws as much as possible, and work really hard. It's not a bad life if only one person you are close to is gone right? Benny was a true friend, a great friend, but certainly he can live his life without him. He grew up without him, so he can finish college and start his career without him as well. Yeah, that must be what Benny was trying to explain to me this whole time. He knew it was over for him and he just wanted me to be myself, following what I knew to be the best way to live. As he said this over himself, he felt that it was odd, but didn't care to correct himself because it was the only thing that could bring him comfort at this time.

A gentle knock upon the door interrupted Evan's personal monologue. At the door stood Mr. Crib, a brown briefcase in his hands, his suit buttoned and pressed neatly. He input a code into the lock on the door and slowly swung it open.

Looking up, Evan's anger began to emerge as his head started blaming Mr. Crib for everything that had happened to Benny. He let this stuff happen and even kept it going when he probably could have stopped it. Evan began to grind his back teeth together, trying his best to smile and prove that nothing was wrong.

Mr. Crib walked gently through the door, his powerful frame casting an atmosphere of properness and politeness to the room. "Hello, Mr. Roman. You wanted to see me."

Evan was about to shout out, but caught himself and instead, simply said "yes."

"How can I help you?" Mr. Crib continued to ask questions as though Evan was acting like a rabid dog and he wanted to calm him down.

"I, uh, wanted to talk about the contract you gave me," the boy struggled through his sentences.

"Did you have a chance to read it all?" Another gentle question.

"Uh, most of it." Another stuttering answer.

"And how would you like to proceed forward?" Mr. Crib smiled.

Evan swallowed his saliva, which seemed like dropping a heavy stone into his stomach. "I don't think I want the job, sir."

Mr. Crib's smile faded, even to the point of frowning. It was the first time Evan had seen him frown and it didn't look good on him. It made him scary, like he no longer knew what to say next. Despite his looks, however, Mr. Crib politely continued to ask questions.

"Have you read the page about declining the offer of work?"

"I don't remember it."

"Would you like for me to show you where it is?"

"Uh, sure." Evan began to sweat as Mr. Crib's large, powerful hands reached below the small table and pulled his briefcase in front of him.

Opening his briefcase, Mr. Crib pulled out an exact copy of the contract that he had given to Evan the day before. Fingering through the pages, he came to page 87, his eyes following his finger halfway down the page to a section titled: <u>Should the Contract be Declined</u>. "You will want to read this section before you sign the contract declining the job and its benefits," he stated plainly.

Evan stared at the paragraph, reading it to himself while Mr. Crib watched. The language was too wordy, too hard to understand, and far too long for Evan's patience. Eventually, he expressed his frustration.

"Ugh," Evan let out a breath. "There's too much here to understand."

"Would you care for me to give you a short synopsis of the paragraph?"

"Sure."

"It states very clearly that, due to the great benefits of the offer itself, any individual that chooses to decline the offer must come under inspection as their rejecting such an offer would clearly be a sign that they may be acting in ways outside of what is best for themselves and those close to them."

Evan paused, trying to wrap his head around what he heard. "What does that mean?" he finally gave up.

Mr. Crib gathered the contract and began to load it cleanly back into his suitcase. "It says that only someone against the MEBA system would decline the offer, therefore anyone who does decline it should expect that they will have to undergo inspection by the MEBA system. If you reject this offer, I would expect your MEBA score to match Benny's before the end of the week."

"Oh," Evan said under his breath. Suddenly, he felt trapped, unable to speak, think, or move more than an inch in his seat. He began to wonder to himself what he was supposed to do. What could have been minutes went by when he realized that his MEBA by his side was flashing, showing an update to his score.

37.

Mr. Crib, who was looking at Evan peacefully, finally spoke up to break the silence that Evan had found himself stuck in. "Perhaps I can give you another night to think about this rather large decision. I will be here tomorrow morning at 9:30 for your choice. I appreciate your time and wish you good rest."

Evan didn't respond, but watched Mr. Crib pack his suitcase, shut it, lock it, and walk back through the door the same way he entered. When he finally looked back down at the MEBA when Mr. Crib had left, he was surprised to see a 100 staring back at him. Had the MEBA always read 100 and Evan just imagined that it had changed for a moment?

After a moment of collecting his thoughts, Evan looked to see that the Twins were watching him with a book open. "Did you take the job?"

"I wasn't planning on it." Evan wrote back. When he saw the girls read it and give confused faces, he continued. "If I don't take the job, they are going to put me on trial too. The way he said it made it seem like I would be in the same position as Benny since I am basically rejecting the MEBA system."

The girls didn't write anything back, but gave a nod of understanding.

Evan began to pace around the room, talking to himself as he tended to do when he became anxious. The questions rattled around his head as he walked back and forth, every once in a while looking to the twins for feedback; they didn't have any. Everything felt like a puzzle, like a mystery that he had to solve, a way to escape that he hasn't found yet. There had to be a way he could get out of this problem.

He began to feverishly look through his computer, opening up the file that Benny had sent him, looking for something that would help. He no longer cared if opening the file would cause the AMA to look closer at what he was doing. Pouring over it, nothing seemed to stand out; the pattern seemed easy to recognize and simple to put together. The final product still just seemed like an odd little microchip of sorts. Evan couldn't help but feel like it was a dead end.

Next, he started poking through Professor Tile's textbook, hoping that she was connected to Benny more than he knew. He read through most of the chapters on creating microchips, designing them, and how microbiology would interact with them. Nothing came up that looked important. Nothing seemed to connect to what was happening, the number 37, or even the MEBA system. It was just a textbook and another dead end.

Finally, he laid down on his bed and just stared at the ceiling. He had nothing else to say, nothing else to even think about, nothing to live for, nothing else to cry about, nothing to do. With nothing holding his attention, he fell asleep.

CHAPTER 8

Undone

It must have been the middle of the night when Evan woke up. Everything was dark and quiet. His room had been shut down so that he couldn't see outside of it (the usual set up for nighttime). Groggily, he got up and looked around. His MEBA was blinking, inviting him to come and look.:)

As he looked at it, a door slammed from somewhere in the hallway and Evan's eyes rose to meet the sound. Glancing about, noise must have come from the other side of the hallway. Steps, louder and louder, began echoing their way through the corridor. He quickly went to the door, leaving everything but his shoes behind. The lock was blinking as though it was active, but he reached for the handle anyway, hoping the door would be able to open. No luck. The passcode that Mr. Crib had always put in was six digits; Evan had counted it a number of times. He tried his birthday. Nothing. He tried 123456, convincing himself it was worth the effort. Nothing. On the device, instead of giving an error message, it just gave him a smiley face, similar to the one on his MEBA. Evan took a deep breath and put in 37. It wasn't six digits, but he hit enter all the same. The door lock whirled. He swung the door open as quickly as he could with a voice on the other side reacting.

"Whoa, almost hit me." Benny stood in the doorway smiling, still bruised and battered from head to toe. Evan couldn't believe it.

"Aren't you supposed to be…" Evan started crying.

"Oh hey, no time for that," Benny said, grabbing Evan's arm and pulling him outside the room.

Three figures were there, the twins and another gentleman, who Evan almost recognized. He was wearing the same clothes the guards were. The guards! Evan shot a glance around the room, all of the guards were sitting down in their chairs, seemingly asleep.

"Wait, Benny!" He called out as the group began to move down the hall together. Benny didn't wait, but he did slow down so that Evan could catch up. "Is this a dream? Are you really here? Am I going to wake up only to find out that they killed you?"

Benny smiled and kept walking. He, the twins, the gentleman, and Evan stopped in front of the door to the green room. In a moment, the girl who was staying there walked out of her room, dressed far too formally for whatever situation this was. Evan thought to himself that she seemed ready to audition to be a news broadcaster. Even in the darkness of the night, he could tell she was strikingly beautiful.

"Benny!" Evan whispered loud enough for everyone to hear. "Are the guards dead?"

He didn't respond, only turned to the group, looked them in the eyes, and said "The elevator is shut down for now. We will have to go this way." Suddenly, Evan knew this was his dream again. He let out a sigh and began looking for more clues, something to help him figure out what was going on at the AMA or with Benny.

Down the long hallway, the group walked quickly towards Mr. Crib's desk and past it, heading up to the door where Evan had originally gotten his job offer. He knew that Benny would open the door, just like his last dream. He knew that Benny would tell everyone else to go first.

The spiral staircase just beyond the door stared at Benny, a light above it flickering in the darkness, beckoning him to end his dream by walking towards it. One by one the group went up, the leader of them holding the door so they could rush through. The twins went first; the dream seemed to show Benny that they were each holding something. Diane was holding something like a small electric box while Celeste had a sort of piece of clear, thick paper. Every once in a while, the girls would hold up one of their objects and a few seconds later, they would begin to move with more and more purpose. Next went the beautiful girl, managing the spiral staircase in her heels very well. On her back, he saw a tattoo peeking out behind the purple dress suit she was wearing. It looked a little bit like Egyptian hieroglyphics. Finally, the gentleman came into the light of the stairwell, his guard outfit was neatly pressed and fit cleanly on his shoulders. In his mind, Evan pictured the face of the fidgeting guard, the one he had laughed at so many times in his head. If it was him, why was he helping? Evan felt as though he was missing out on something important; he had to ask Benny later what had happened and why these people were all here.

It was finally Evan's turn. He didn't want the dream to end. Turning to Benny, he asked another question, trying to get as much information as he could before he woke up. "Hey Benny, do you think they would really have tried to kill you?"

His friend shot him a curious look, which was almost comical through all of the bruises and scars marking his face. As though giving in to his friend after he had begged him to do something crazy, Benny chuckled and looked straight into Evan's eyes. "You were asleep for a long time. Come on, it's your turn. Go."

Evan started up the staircase, the light above giving him just enough not to fall or miss a step. He recognized that the dream was continuing, so he took in every detail he could: eleven steps per floor, three floors up, beige walls. The other four members of the group had already stopped at the top of the staircase when Evan arrived a few moments later. When Benny arrived, the gentleman took out his keys and opened the door.

The morning light was just coming out over the tall hill behind the old school building, illuminating everyone's faces. Benny was the last one out and he let out a very happy shout when he stepped onto the dirt. All of the others started laughing and shouting and celebrating along with him; even Evan began to jump and laugh, but he wasn't really sure why. It was an odd way for him to act, but he certainly enjoyed it. In the briefest moment, he stopped to wonder if they should be running away since they were still so close to the building, but that fear dissolved as he watched Benny join in the celebration. If he was up for it, Evan decided that there wasn't a reason to stop.

Eventually, as the group calmed down and took in the sunrise, Evan couldn't help but ask his questions. "What the heck is going on Benny?"

"I've been looking forward to this for a long time. I knew you would make the right choice."

"Just tell me what happened!" Evan shouted at his friend, immediately feeling badly for his outrage.

Everyone around him just laughed at it, as though Evan was being pranked and they finally got to show him. Benny pulled him to the side, far enough away for them to talk on their own.

"I did it," he smiled through his bruises. "I stopped the MEBA system."

"How? They were planning on killing you tonight. Did you escape?"

Benny looked around himself at the dirt and the nearby grassy hill and the sun. "It seems so." He laughed. "Evan, they carried out the sentence yesterday; you were asleep the whole time." At this, he unbuttoned his messy, wrinkled shirt. Across his chest was a scar larger than a hand and a small lump in the middle of it sticking out. It was gross to first see, but still very cool, Evan thought.

"What happened?" Evan sighed.

"The blueprints. Did you figure out what they were for?"

"It was a microchip of some sort, right?"

"Yes, and..?"

"It was meant to be inserted into a MEBA somewhere?"

"Good! Yes."

"That's all I got."

"Slap me," Benny said straight-faced. Evan just stared. "Seriously, if you want to know what happened, you will have to slap me."

"I think you are hurt enough."

"Come on, you can do it."

Evan slapped his friend, not too hard, but hard enough to hurt. Then he realized that it would probably trigger his MEBA score and immediately apologized. His heart was racing, a tell-tale sign of guilt.

"Now what?" Evan couldn't help himself.

"Exactly. Remember that device I was working on before the blueprints?"

"The one that shut down my MEBA?"

"The microchip had that code built into it. I had put it inside my chest where the MEBA is inserted. I knew that if they found me guilty of trying to overthrow the system, they would try to kill me by shutting down my heart with an electrical pulse."

"So you had the microchip intercept the signal and instead of killing you, it killed the system?" Evan finally put it together.

"Bingo."

"So you really did want to be found guilty."

"It was the only way to ensure I had access to the mainframe of their system. I couldn't dismantle it otherwise."

"So it's all gone? Is the whole MEBA system destroyed?"

"Not really. The system still functions."

"What's the point? I thought you wanted to destroy the system."

"Nope. I just wanted to change a small part of it."

"So what actually changed? Is guilt still reported? Will scores matter?"

"Yes and no. Everything for people will stay roughly the same, except that their scores will all be nullified. The system will still report the guilty action, but instead of going into the system to be filed, it will now just get redirected."

"Where?"

Benny just pointed to his chest, where the microchip had been implanted. Evan stood for a few seconds with his jaw to the floor.

Finally, Evan continued to ask questions. "Will it hurt or affect you?"

"Yes, but I can take it." Benny smiled wide through the bruises. "I'm pretty tough."

"Will I still feel guilt?"

"Yes, but it will only reassure you of what you already know. It won't report anything, nor be kept on record. The microchip in me actually completely deletes it as soon as it processes. You might still feel the guilt, but there's no guilt that will ever be processed again. I removed it's ability to affect you."

"What about the AMA?"

"What about them?"

"Were they bad?"

"Not in the way that you would normally think."

Evan stood there in silence, waiting for Benny to explain. When he didn't explain, Evan continued to fill in the gaps he had mulled over so much in his own head. "So no more MEBA scores?"

"Nope."

"How do you think the world will handle that?"

Benny put his bruised arm around his friend's shoulder and led him back to the group, which at this point had made it up to the top of the hill. When he got to the top, he started to speak to the five of them.

"How the world responds to this will vary. A handful of people will outright deny that it happened, cover up or re-make the system as best they can. They will try to go back to the safety of knowing exactly where they stand compared to everyone else because of a score. Others will take this and say that what they do no longer matters. They will hurt each other because they will kill that good feeling of knowing what is wrong and when they can't feel their own pain, they won't care about hurting others."

"That's terrible," Diane blurted out.

"It will be yes. But they were just lying to themselves about how good they were anyway. This will just be the next step they would have taken all along if the MEBA system weren't in place."

The man in the guard's uniform spoke up, kind and gentle in his voice. "Will people be able to be good anymore?"

Benny laughed a bit. "I haven't changed morality, you know. Only how it is measured. Much of the world won't like having the MEBA system gone because it means they will lose control over the hearts and minds of people. A few people, however, will love it, because they will no longer be measured by how many good and bad actions they take."

Evan finally piped up from underneath his friend's arm. "How will they be measured? Is there another way for people to know if they are good enough for society?"

Benny removed his arm from around Evan, walked a little further and stopped. He turned around, his bruises and scars colorful in the morning sun. He saw how much his friend had fought for him, wrestled, doubted, cried, and over-thought for him. A huge smile, bigger than the one he had been wearing, burst forth. His eyebrows raised as he spoke.

"Come this way."

Made in United States
Orlando, FL
27 July 2023

35507517R00082